Katie

and the

cupcake

war

SIMON SPOTLIGHT

An imprint of Simon & Schuster Children's Publishing Division

1230 Avenue of the Americas, New York, New York 10020

Copyright © 2012 by Simon & Schuster, Inc. All rights reserved, including the right of reproduction in whole or in part in any form.

SIMON SPOTLIGHT and colophon are registered trademarks of Simon & Schuster, Inc.

Text by Tracey West

Chapter header illustrations by Ana Benaroya

Designed by Laura Roode

For information about special discounts for bulk purchases, please contact Simon & Schuster Special Sales at 1-866-506-1949 or business@simonandschuster.com.

Manufactured in the United States of America 0617 OFF

First Edition 10 9 8 7 6

ISBN 978-1-4424-5373-9

ISBN 978-1-4424-5374-6 (eBook)

Library of Congress Catalog Card Number 2012936360

CUPCAKE DIARIES

Katie
and the
cupcake
war

by coco simon

Simon Spotlight

New York London Toronto Sydney New Delhi

CHAPTER 1

You Are *Not* Going to Believe This!

"Mia! Is it really you? I haven't seen you in a gazillion years!" I cried, hugging my friend.

Mia laughed. "Katie, I was only gone for, like, four days," she said.

"That is four days, ninety-six hours, or five thousand, seven hundred, and sixty minutes," I said. Then I dramatically put my hand over my heart. "I know, because I counted them all."

"I missed you too," Mia said. "But you couldn't have missed me too much. You were trying out new recipes with the techniques you learned at cooking camp, weren't you?"

"Yes," I told her, "but it felt like you were gone forever. I almost didn't recognize you!"

Actually, I was kidding. Mia looked pretty much

the same, with her straight black hair and dark eyes. She might have gotten a little bit tanner from her long weekend at the beach. She was wearing white shorts and a white tank top with a picture of a pink cupcake on it.

"Hey, I just noticed your shirt!" I said. "That's so cool!"

Mia smiled. "I made it at camp. One of the counselors there was totally into fashion, and she showed me how do this computer thing where you can turn your drawing into a T-shirt design."

I was definitely impressed. "You drew that? It's awesome."

"Thanks," Mia said. "I was thinking maybe I could make T-shirts for the Cupcake Club, for when we go on jobs. You know, so we could all dress alike."

Now it was my turn to laugh. We all like to bake cupcakes, but when it comes to fashion, the members of the Cupcake Club don't have much in common. "Well, I know we all wore matching sweatshirts when we won our first baking contest," I said. "But that was a special occasion. I don't know if you could create one T-shirt we would all be happy wearing on a semiregular basis."

Then the doorbell rang. It was Emma and

Alexis, and what they were wearing proved my point. Emma is a real "girlie girl," although I don't mean that in a bad way, it just describes Emma really well. Pink is her favorite color, and I don't blame her, because pink looks really nice on you when you have blond hair and blue eyes like Emma does. She wore a pink sundress with tiny white flowers on it and pink flip-flops to match her dress.

Alexis had her curly red hair pulled back in a scrunchie, and she wore a light blue tennis shirt and jean shorts with white sneakers. And I might as well tell you what I was wearing: a yellow T-shirt from my cooking camp signed by all the kids who went there, ripped jeans with iron-on patches, and bare feet, because I was in my house, after all. Oh, and I painted each of my toenails a different color when I was bored.

"Mia! I missed you!" Emma cried, giving Mia a hug.

"So how was your first vacation with your mom, Eddie, and Dan?" Alexis asked. Eddie and Dan are Mia's stepdad and stepbrother, respectively.

"Pretty good," Mia replied. "The beach house was nice, and we got to play a lot of volleyball. And the boardwalk food was delicious."

"That reminds me," I said. "Follow me to the kitchen, guys."

My cooking camp experience had inspired me to surprise my friends for our Cupcake Club meeting. I had covered the kitchen table with my favorite tablecloth, a yellow one with orange and red flowers with green leaves. (Mom says she needs to wear sunglasses to eat when we use it, but I love the bright colors. Plus, they reminded me of the colors of Mexico, and it matched all the food I had made.)

Laid out on the table was a bowl of bright green guacamole, a platter of enchiladas with red sauce on top, homemade tortilla chips, a pitcher of fresh lemonade, and a plate of tiny cupcakes, each one topped with a dollop of whipped cream and sprinkled with cinnamon.

My friends gasped, and I felt really proud.

"Katie, this looks amazingly fantastic!" Mia said. "Did you make all this yourself?"

I nodded. "We had Mexican day in cooking camp, and I learned how to do all this stuff," I said. I pointed to the mini cupcakes. "Those are *tres leches* cupcakes."

"Three milks," Mia translated. "Those are sweet and delicious. My *abuela* makes a *tres leches* cake when somebody has a birthday."

I nodded. "Emma, I thought they might be good for the bridal shop."

One of the Cupcake Club's biggest clients is the The Special Day bridal shop. We make mini cupcakes that they give to their customers, and the only requirement is that the frosting has to be white. Emma usually helps delivers them. She has even modeled the bridesmaids dresses at the bridal shop too. (I told you she was a girlie girl.)

"They look perfect!" Emma agreed. "So pretty. And I bet they taste as good as they look."

"Then let's start eating so you can find out," I suggested. "I think the enchiladas are getting cold."

Then my mom walked into the kitchen. She has brown hair, like me, but hers is curly, and today it was all messy. She looked tired, but I thought maybe it was because she had patients all morning. She's a dentist and has to work a lot.

"Oh, girls, you're here!" she said. "Alexis, how was your trip to the shore?"

"Actually, Mia's the one who went to beach," Alexis answered politely. "But thanks for asking."

Mom blushed. "Sorry, girls. I'm exhausted. My head feels like it's full of spaghetti today."

"That's okay, Mrs. Brown," Mia said. "I had a good time."

Then the phone rang. "That's probably your grandmother," Mom said to me. "Come find me if you need anything, okay?"

"Shmpf," I replied. Actually, I was saying "sure," but my mouth was full of guacamole.

Alexis took a chip and dipped it in the guacamole.

"Wow, that's really good," she remarked when she was done chewing. (Unlike me, Alexis doesn't ever talk with her mouth full.)

"Thanks," I said. "Guacamole is my new favorite food. I could eat it all day. Guacamole on pancakes, guacamole pizza for dinner . . ."

"Guacamole-and-jelly sandwiches for lunch," Mia said, giggling.

"Gross!" Emma squealed.

"I think I'll stick to guacamole and chips," Alexis said matter-of-factly. Then she wiped her hands on a napkin and opened up her notebook. Alexis loves to get down to business at a Cupcake Club meeting.

"Okay. So, I was looking at our client list," she began. "The only thing on our schedule this fall is our usual gig at The Special Day. We need to drum up some new business. I was thinking that we could send out a postcard to everyone who's ever ordered cupcakes from us. You know, something like 'Summer's Over, and Cupcake Season Has Started.'"

"I like it," I said. Emma and Mia nodded in agreement.

"That reminds me," Mia said, pointing to her shirt. "I designed this. I could make a T-shirt for each of us. I thought we could wear them when we go on jobs."

"Oh, it's so cute!" Emma said. "Could my shirt be pink?"

Mia smiled. "I guess so. We could each have a different color shirt if we want. Unless you want it to be more like a uniform."

"Or we could expand our business and sell the T-shirts, too," Alexis said, sounding excited. "I bet we could find a site online where we could get the shirts made cheaply, and sell them for a profit."

Mia frowned a little bit. "I don't know, Alexis. I was thinking these should just be for us, you know? Special."

"But you want to be a fashion designer, don't you?" Alexis asked. "This could be the start of your business. Mia's Cupcake Clothing!"

Mia looked thoughtful, and I couldn't tell if she liked the idea or not. I decided to change the subject. If Mia decided she was interested, she'd bring up the idea again. Sometimes Alexis can get a little pushy when she wants the club to do something. Which is mostly good, because otherwise we'd never get anything done.

"Wow, I can't believe school is starting so soon." Then I said with a nod to Emma and Alexis, "Though what I really still can't believe is Sydney's singing routine at your day camp's talent show. It's in my nightmares."

When I first started middle school last year, Sydney Whitman made my life miserable. So I didn't feel bad about making fun of her—well, not *too* bad, anyway. My grandma Carole says that two wrongs don't make a right, and she's got a point. But Sydney really made my life miserable.

"Oh my gosh, I can't believe I forgot to tell you!" Emma said. "I have big news. *Huge!* You guys are *not* going to believe this!"

"Tell us what?" I asked.

"It's about Sydney," Emma said. "Sydney's mom returned a bunch of library books and told my mom that they were moving—to California!"

"No WAY!" I cried, jumping out of my chair. "Are you serious?"

Emma nodded. "I'm pretty sure they moved already. Sydney's dad got transferred to some company in San Diego or something. Sydney's mom said they had to move immediately for Sydney to start school there on time."

I started jumping up and down and waving my hands in the air.

"Look out, everyone. Katie's doing her happy dance," Mia said.

"This is awesome! Amazing! Stupendous! Wonderful! Did I say awesome?" I cried. "No more Sydney! No more Popular Girls Club to ruin our lives!"

"Well, actually, I'm sure the PGC will continue," Alexis replied. "They've still got Maggie and Bella and Callie. I bet Callie will become their new leader."

I felt like a balloon that somebody just popped. One of the reasons Sydney made my life miserable last year was because she took my best friend, Callie, away from me. Yes, I know that nobody forced Callie to dump me and become a member of the PGC. But it was always easier to blame Sydney than to get mad at Callie. Callie and I have been friends since we were babies.

Oh, and the Popular Girls Club is just what it sounds like. It's a club Sydney started where they invite popular girls to join. They do everything together. I started to get so mad just thinking about it, then I realized Mia was talking to me.

"So Callie didn't mention any of this to you?" Mia asked.

"No!" I said, feeling a little exasperated. "I mean, I barely talk to her anymore."

I know I shouldn't get so freaked out about Callie. If she hadn't dumped me, I probably never would have become friends with Mia, Emma, and Alexis. There would be no Cupcake Club. But something happened to Callie when she got into middle school. Sometimes she could be not so nice. So it was probably for the best that we weren't friends. We saw each other when our families got together—our moms are best friends, and, yes, that gets really weird—but that was about it.

Anyway, I must admit, there was a little part of me that hoped, now that Sydney was gone, that Callie would be friends with me again. I imagined her showing up at the front door.

Oh, Katie, I have treated you so badly, she would say. *Can I please join your Cupcake Club?*

Of course, I would say, trying to be the better person. *I forgive you, Callie.*

Then again, that would make things pretty confusing, because Mia was my best friend now, and I'm not sure how this would all work. Now *my* head felt like it was full of spaghetti. (Although I would never say that out loud, because that is such a weird mom thing to say.)

"Earth to Katie," Mia said. "You there?"

I snapped myself out of my fantasy. "Sorry. I must be in a guacamole haze," I said, taking my seat. "Okay. Enough about the PGC. Let's get down to business."

Maybe Alexis had the right idea after all.

CHAPTER 2

What Was *That* All About?

$\mathcal{O}$nce I stopped worrying about what Callie was going to do, I spent the next few days on a Sydney-free cloud of happiness. A world without Sydney was a world filled with rainbows, cotton candy, and sunshine every day. I didn't even get nervous about my first day of school.

Any normal person would have been nervous. Last year, the first day of middle school was one of the worst days of my life. I lost my best friend, got in trouble for using my cell phone, couldn't open my locker, and couldn't find my way around the school and was nearly late getting to every class.

But this year, things started out amazingly great. When I got on the bus, Mia was sitting in our usual seat in the sixth row from the front, saving it for me, just like always.

"Hey, you're wearing your lucky purple shirt," Mia said as I slid into my seat. She always notices what I'm wearing.

"Yeah, I need all the luck I can get," I said. "I do not want this year's first day of school to be like last year's."

Mia made a fake-hurt face. "Hey, you met me on the first day of school last year."

"That was the only good thing, believe me," I said. Then I remembered. "Besides meeting Alexis and Emma, too."

Then Mia noticed my hands. "Cool nails."

I wiggled my fingers. I had painted each fingernail in a different color this time. "For extra luck!"

"You don't need luck, Katie," Mia said. "You know how to do stuff this time. You'll be fine."

"I hope so," I said.

Then a boy with brown hair looked over the seat behind us. It was George Martinez, a kid I've known since elementary school. George always says a lot of funny stuff that makes me laugh. Sometimes he teases me, which is annoying, but he's still kind of funny. He was sitting next to his friend Ken Watanabe, as usual.

"Hi, Katie," he said. "How was the rest of your summer?"

George has never asked me a normal question like that before. For a second I didn't know what to say. I was trying to think of a funny reply, because I can usually make George laugh.

Then Mia nudged me, and I realized I was staring into space like a zombie again.

"Um, good," I finally answered.

"That's good," George said. Then he sat back down.

Mia leaned over to whisper into my ear. "He *so* likes you!"

"Sshhh!" I warned her. If George heard her, that would be so embarrassing. Mostly because I think I kind of like George, even though I'm not entirely sure what that's supposed to feel like. And if he liked me back, it might be awesome or it might be very weird.

Then the bus arrived at Park Street Middle School, a big U-shaped school made of bricks the color of sand. Before I climbed up the front steps with Mia, I stopped and got my schedule out of the front pocket of my backpack. I knew my homeroom class was in room number 322, but I wanted to make sure.

Just then Emma and Alexis walked up. They both live a few blocks away from the school, so they don't have to take the bus.

"Katie! Hooray! Now we can go to homeroom together," Emma said.

"Oh yeah! I forgot," I admitted. A few nights ago, we had all texted our schedules to one another to see if we were in the same classes together. Last year, I didn't have any friends in my homeroom class. I smiled. "Hey, I'm really lucky that you're in my homeroom. My good luck shirt must be working."

"*And* your good luck nail polish," Mia reminded me.

The front of the school was starting to get crowded, so I said good-bye to Alexis and Mia, and Emma and I headed to homeroom. We got to room 322 without getting lost, because we knew our way around the school already.

Inside the room we were greeted by these words written on the board: WELCOME, STUDENTS! GET READY FOR A MATH ADVENTURE! MR. KAZINSKI. The teacher sitting behind the desk at the front of the room was a tall man with sandy-blond hair and glasses. The walls around the room were decorated with posters that said stuff like "Believe

You Can Achieve," and others had math symbols on them.

Emma and I found seats in the row by the window before the bell rang. Mr. Kazinski stood up and smiled at us.

"Hey, it's good to see everyone today," he said. "I've got some announcements, but first, the news."

Right then Principal LaCosta's voice came over the PA speaker.

"Good morning, everyone, and welcome to the first day of school at Park Street," she said. "I can tell it's going to be a wonderful year. Let's start out by saying the Pledge of Allegiance together."

After the pledge, Mr. Kazinski started talking again. "By now you've guessed that my name is Mr. Kazinski, but you guys can call me Mr. K.," he said. "You'll see me for ten minutes every morning here in homeroom, and if you are taking my math class, you'll see me for forty minutes more."

I glanced at my schedule. I had math next, in this very room, with Mr. K. More good luck! I don't love math, but I already liked Mr. K. My math teacher last year, Mrs. Moore, was okay but she was pretty strict and not very friendly. She was a cloudy day compared to Mr. K.'s sunny day, if you know what I mean.

Another point for my lucky purple shirt, I thought happily.

And I got even luckier because even though I had to say good-bye to Emma after home-room, Mia walked into the room. We had math together!

The morning just seemed to get better and better. My second-period class, Spanish, was just down the hall. Then I went to gym class, and I was so happy—Emma, Mia, and Alexis were there!

I should probably explain my history with gym, or "physical education," as teachers like to call it. I'm a pretty fast runner, but when it comes to most other sports stuff, I'm sort of a spaz. When we play volleyball and I hit the ball, I usually end up hitting the wall or the ceiling or a person. It's not pretty. And last year, I got teased pretty hard about it.

I *am* good at softball, though. I even made the school team. But I like playing for fun. I'm not competitive, and being on a team that always played to win stressed me out too much, so I gave it up.

This year, though, I would have my three best friends to back me up in gym class. And I knew I would need it, because I had the same gym teacher, Ms. Chen. She acts more like an army drill sergeant than a middle school teacher. Honestly, she scares me.

Since it was the first day of school, we didn't have to change into our gym clothes or anything. So before the bell rang, we were all just kind of hanging out on the bleachers. Some of the boys were running around and throwing basketballs at one another.

One of the balls bounced right up to where I was sitting with my friends. It rolled to my feet, so I picked it up, and George Martinez ran over to get it.

"Hey, Silly Arms! We're in the same class again," he said, smiling.

George started calling me Silly Arms last year, because of the way I play volleyball. I've never looked in a mirror while playing volleyball, but I guess I must look pretty silly. I never get mad because I know he's just teasing, like he always does. But then some other kids (like Sydney and her friends, for instance) started calling me that to be mean.

Before I could say anything to George, Eddie Rossi ran up behind him. Eddie is the tallest kid in our grade, and probably in our whole school. Last year he even grew a mustache. But I guess he shaved it over the summer, because his face looked clean-shaven again.

Anyway, this is what Eddie said: "Hey, leave her alone!"

"It's okay," George replied. "Katie's cool!"

Then he took the ball from me and tossed it to Eddie, and they both ran off.

My mouth was open so wide, you could probably have fit a whole cupcake into it.

"That was weird," I said.

"It's so obvious," Alexis said. "Eddie likes you."

"No way," I told her. "It makes no sense. Last year Eddie teased me just as bad as Sydney did. He used to call me Silly Arms all the time. Besides, he's a jock who likes popular girls, not girls like me."

"That doesn't mean he can't still like you," Alexis argued. "People change all the time. He doesn't even have a mustache anymore."

"Well, I think that Eddie and George *both* like Katie," Mia said.

I must have been blushing, because my face

felt hot. I am not the kind of girl who boys get a crush on, and especially not *two* boys at once.

Then Ms. Chen marched in, blowing her whistle, and for once I was glad to see her.

"Stand up and look alive, people! Just because it's the first day of school doesn't mean you can be slackers!"

I jumped to my feet pretty quickly. You definitely don't want Ms. Chen on your case. But I couldn't stop wondering about what happened with Eddie and George and if it meant I was still having good luck or not.

CHAPTER 3

This Means War!

$\mathcal{M}$s. Chen spent the whole gym period telling us the rules of gym and giving us advice about fitness. Finally, the bell rang.

"That was totally boring, but definitely better than being hit in the head by a volleyball," I told my friends as we left. Everyone laughed.

"Don't worry. I'm sure that will happen next week," Mia teased me.

"Hey, we can all go to lunch together," Emma realized.

"I'm going to stop at my locker first," I said. "This math book is pretty heavy. I don't want to carry it around all afternoon."

"No problem, we can all meet at our table, like always," Mia said.

I liked the sound of that. On the first day of school last year, I didn't know where to sit. Now I had three good friends to sit with. I would definitely call that lucky!

Last year I was convinced that my locker was an evil robot out to get me. It's one of those lockers where the lock is built into the door, and the school gives you the combination. I swear I always put in the right one, but that locker never wanted to open.

So I took a deep breath as I slowly turned the dial.

26 . . . 14 . . . 5 . . .

I pulled the handle, and the door wouldn't open.

Oh no! It's happening again! I thought. My heart began to beat faster. I took another deep breath and turned again.

26 . . . 14 . . . 5 . . .

Click! I pulled the handle, and the door opened up.

"Thank you, lucky fingernails," I whispered.

Then I noticed the two girls at the lockers next to me. They were talking pretty loudly.

"It's true! Sydney really moved!" one girl said.

"Does this mean no more PGC?" the other girl asked.

As I headed to the lunchroom, I heard more kids talking.

"I heard the PGC broke up."

"I heard that Sydney left Maggie in charge."

"I wonder if they'll let me join now."

I kind of couldn't believe how many people were talking about Sydney. She was miles away, and she was still the most popular person in school. In a way, that's kind of impressive.

Mia, Emma, Alexis, and I ended up in the cafeteria together at the same time. We made our way to our favorite table, near the back of the room. Alexis and Emma put down their backpacks and went to get on the lunch line. Mia and I always bring lunch from home, so we opened up our lunch bags.

"Did your mom pack you a back-to-school cupcake?" Mia asked.

"Probably," I said. There's been a special cupcake in my first school lunch ever since I could remember.

But when I opened up my bag, I found a turkey and guacamole wrap, an apple, a bag of carrot sticks, and my water bottle—but no cupcake.

"That's weird," I said. "Maybe she forgot to put it in." I felt pretty disappointed.

Suddenly a strange hush came over the noisy

cafeteria, and Mia and I both looked up to see what was going on.

My former best friend, Callie, was walking through the cafeteria with Maggie and Bella, the other two members of the PGC. Even though they all look different—Callie is tall with blond hair and blue eyes; Maggie is kind of short with crazy, curly brown hair; and Bella (her real name is Brenda) has dark hair and tries to look like that girl from those vampire movies—they were all dressed kind of the same. They each had on short-sleeved sweaters, plaid skirts, dark tights, and ankle boots.

"Those outfits are straight out of last month's *Teen Style*," Mia observed.

"Isn't it kind of warm for sweaters?" I wondered. "It's still officially summer, you know."

The three of them casually walked to the PGC's usual table, but you could tell they knew everyone was looking at them. Then Alexis and Emma came back to our table with their lunch trays.

"Well, I guess the PGC is still going strong," Alexis remarked.

"*Everyone's* talking about it," Emma said as she sat down.

"I know," I told them. "It's kind of crazy."

"Anyway, I have way more exciting news than

24

that," Alexis said. "We haven't even gotten our fly-ers out yet, but I booked a job today. Ms. Biddle stopped me in the hallway. She wants some cup-cakes for a birthday party in a couple of months."

Ms. Biddle was our science teacher last year, and one of our first customers. She's really cool.

"Awesome," I said. "I wonder what kind she wants?"

"Before we talk about that, we should talk about this year's school fund-raiser," Alexis said. "I so want to win again."

I took a bite of my turkey wrap and nodded. At the start of the year, the school has this big fair right before the first school dance, and school groups have booths and try to raise money for the school. Last year our cupcake booth raised the most money, and we won. The PGC did this awful makeover booth, and it felt kind of good to beat them.

"Last year we did the school colors and went with vanilla cupcakes," Alexis reminded us. "I'm thinking that we need to switch it up this year."

Mia nodded. "Yeah, we can do something really creative."

We all got excited thinking of what we could do.

"How about a big tower of cupcakes?" Emma suggested.

"Cool!" I cried. "Or maybe we could do the world's biggest cupcake and sell pieces of it."

"Then we would need the world's biggest oven," Alexis pointed out.

"Maybe we could think of a theme, and then we could decorate the booth in the theme and do cupcakes to match," Mia said.

We really liked that idea. "But what kind of theme?" I asked. "It should have something to do with school, right?"

We were so busy talking that I didn't notice when Callie walked up to the table, followed by Maggie and Bella.

"Hey, Katie," she said, and I jumped a little at the sound of my name.

"Oh hey, Callie," I said, although what I really wanted to say was, *What on Earth are you doing at our table?*

"So, I was just wondering if you guys are going to do cupcakes for the fund-raiser this year," she said.

Alexis looked straight at her. "Well," she said, "we're the Cupcake Club. It's kind of a given."

Callie ignored her. "Well, we were thinking of doing cupcakes this year."

I almost choked on my carrot stick. The PGC

could *not* do cupcakes! That was copying! I was about to start freaking out when Mia spoke up in her usual calm, cool way.

"I guess may the best cupcake win, then," she said.

Callie got a look on her face, like maybe she wasn't expecting that answer. Like maybe she *wanted* us to freak out. I was glad Mia spoke up first.

"Well, then, I guess it's on," she said, tossing her hair. (And when did she start doing that, anyway?)

Then she turned and walked away, and Maggie and Bella followed her, just like they used to follow Sydney.

"They can't even come up with their own idea!" Alexis fumed.

"'It's on'?" Emma repeated. "What is she even talking about? I thought Callie wasn't as bad as Sydney. She might be worse!"

Mia nodded. "I guess it's clear who the new leader of the PGC is."

I didn't say anything. I couldn't. I felt terrible. It wasn't just the PGC declaring war on the Cupcake Club. It was *Callie* declaring war on *me*. That's what it felt like, anyway. This was the girl I learned to ride bikes with, who I had a zillion sleepovers with, who knew my deepest secrets. I never did anything to make her stop being friends with me, and she dumped me. That was bad enough. But this . . . this really hurt.

I looked down at my rainbow-painted finger-nails.

So much for my lucky day, I thought.

CHAPTER 4

What's Up with Mom?

Even though I was pretty upset by my encounter with Callie, I have to admit that the rest of the day was okay. After lunch, Mia was in my next two classes (which was good, because Callie, Maggie, and Bella were in them too). For fifth period we had social studies with Mrs. Kratzer. She's short, with short hair and round glasses, and she seems really friendly. Then we had science with Ms. Chandar, who's way more serious than Mrs. Kratzer, but she seems nice, too.

In seventh period I had an elective class, and I chose drama for this semester. Even though the idea of getting onstage terrifies me, I didn't have to worry about that in this class. I thought it might be fun to study drama without having to be in a real play, you know? The teacher's name is Mr. Brent, and he looks really young, like he could be in college or something. Anyway, the class looked like it might be fun.

Finally, I had English. English is my favorite subject, so it's like saving the best for last. The teacher, Ms. Harmeyer, seems kind of quiet and shy, like somebody who likes to read books all the time instead of talking a lot. I guess maybe that's why she became an English teacher.

When school ended, I packed all my books into my backpack and went outside to catch the bus. Last year, Joanne, who works in my mom's office, would pick me up and take me to Mom's work until her day was over. Some days my mom gets off early, and some days she has to work late.

This year, Mom said I could take the bus home and stay at the house by myself. I almost couldn't believe it. My mom has always been superprotective, probably because she's had to raise me by herself. I figured she wouldn't let me stay by myself until I graduated college. But now I have my own key to the house, and it feels pretty cool.

When I got home I headed right for the kitchen and ate a banana. I forgot how hungry going to school makes me!

Then I remembered that I was supposed to call Mom the second I got in the door. Whoops! I was a little surprised Mom hadn't called or alerted the fire department when she didn't hear from me.

"Hi, sweetie!" Mom said when she picked up. "How was the first day of school?"

"Well," I said, unsure of how much I wanted to tell her about Callie, "mostly it was pretty good."

"Great!" she said. "Can't wait to hear all about it when I get home. Now please begin your homework, okay? I'll be home to start dinner soon."

I hung up. The house was quiet and empty, so I decided to go to my room and blast my iPod while I did my homework.

My room is kind of small, but it has everything I need in it. The furniture is this white bedroom set that was my mom's when she was a little girl, and Grandma Carole and Grandpa Chuck saved it in case Mom ever had a little girl of her own—me! A few years ago I started putting stickers on everything, and Mom got a little mad, but then Grandma Carole told her it was my set now, and it should reflect my personality. My grandma is pretty cool that way.

During the summer I used some of my Cupcake Club earnings to get stuff for my room that I saw in a catalog. Over my desk there's a big cupcake-shaped bulletin board that I can stick pictures on. There are two pink cupcake-shaped pillows on top of my purple-and-green bedspread too.

I try to keep my room neat, but mostly I end up sticking things in the closet. Then when I can't shut the door, I have to clean everything up before Mom sees it. Luckily, I had just done that before school started, so things were looking pretty nice.

I opened my backpack, put all my books on top of my desk, and then turned on the laptop Grandma Carole and Grandpa Chuck got me for my last birthday. Then I plugged my iPod into the dock on the nightstand next to my bed and turned it all the way up.

Mom never would have let me play music so loud during homework time, so it felt pretty daring. I didn't really have much to do anyway, since it was the first day of school. Ms. Harmeyer's assignment was to write a poem about one thing you did this summer. I think my poems always end up sounding corny, so I decided to wait until Mom came home to help me. She was really good at writing stuff. Instead I went online to look up some cupcake ideas for the fund-raiser.

I got distracted by all the ads for cupcake supplies that kept popping up, and before I knew it, it was five forty-five. I thought that was weird, because Mom always gets home by five thirty on the dot.

A few minutes later I heard Mom's voice calling up the stairs.

"Katie! Turn that down!"

I quickly ran to shut off the iPod and then bounded down the steps. Mom was at the bottom wearing jeans and a white blouse, which was also weird because she always wears her scrubs home.

"Hey, you're late," I said. "Did you have an emergency at work?"

"Katie, I told you, I didn't go to work today," Mom said. "I had to take Grandma Carole to the doctor again."

"Um, no, you did not tell me that," I said. "Is she okay?"

"We'll talk about it at dinner, Katie," Mom replied. "I ordered us a pizza. It'll be here soon."

I couldn't believe it. Mom and I had pizza last night. Normally, Mom won't even let us order pizza. She makes it herself, including the crust. And when we do order it in, she makes us get veggies on top of it. So delivery pizza two nights in a row was totally out of the ordinary.

"But we just had pizza last night," I reminded her.

Mom sighed. "I'm sorry, Katie. I forgot."

"How could you forget?" I asked. "Remember, we got eggplant and black olives for the very first time, and you said it was the best pizza yet."

Mom motioned me over to the couch. "Katie, let's talk now. You should know what's going on," she said. She sounded superserious, and I felt a little scared.

I sat down next to her.

"Katie, it looks like Grandma Carole is going to have surgery for her heart," Mom said. "The doctors say she's going to be fine. She's in really good health. You know how active she is."

I nodded. "She's better at sports than I am."

"But she has a lot of doctor's appointments to go to, and Grandpa Chuck is still having trouble with his knees, so I'm going to take her," Mom explained. Grandma Carole lives, like, an hour away, so I knew that wasn't going to be easy. "And then, when she goes in for her surgery . . ."

The doorbell rang—it was the pizza guy. While Mom paid for the food, I thought about what she had just said. It sounded serious, but Mom said Grandma was going to be okay. Moms don't lie about that stuff, do they?

I set the table, and soon we were eating broccoli pizza and salad. It was so delicious, I didn't mind we were having pizza for the second day in a row.

"This is sooo good," I said, swallowing a bite of pizza. "I was starving after school today."

Mom threw down her napkin. "Oh, Katie, I almost forgot! How was the first day of school?"

"It was pretty good," I said. I told her most of the stuff that happened. I left out the part about Eddie and George, because that was kind of embarrassing. And I didn't tell her about Callie, because I didn't want her to get upset. I also left out the part about the missing cupcake, because now I understood why she forgot about it.

"Well, it sounds like you're off to a good start," Mom said with a smile, and then her look got serious. "Katie, we still need to talk about the surgery. I'm going to have to stay with Grandma Carole a few days while she's recovering. Mrs. Rogers is going to stay with you."

Mom announced it in that fake-happy voice adults use when they are trying to convince you that what they are saying is good when they really know it isn't. I almost groaned out loud.

Mrs. Rogers is the woman who took care of me when I was a little kid and Mom had to work. She still babysits me sometimes when Mom goes out late, and the annoying thing is that she still treats me like a three-year-old. The last time she was here, she actually checked my toothbrush before I went to bed to make sure I had brushed my teeth. My mom is a dentist! Of *course* I brushed my teeth!

"Mom, not Mrs. Rogers, please," I begged. "She treats me like a baby. Can't I go with you?"

"Absolutely not," Mom said. "You need to stay in school."

I bit my lip. "But, Mom, it's not fair!"

"Katie, I really need your cooperation here," Mom said, and I could tell I had upset her. "I don't want to worry about you while I'm taking care of Grandma. So no complaining, okay?"

It was really, really hard not to say anything back, but I kept quiet. I knew Mom was right. I would just have to deal with Mrs. Rogers for a few days. Thank goodness for school.

But I was still feeling kind of bad. Then I remembered something from Ms. Chen's boring fitness lecture that actually made me feel better.

"Mom, the lights on the high school track stay

on until nine," I said. "Can we go for a run?"

The worried look on Mom's face relaxed. "Why not? Let's wait a little bit. It's not good to go running right after you eat. But I think a run would do us both good."

So a little while later I changed into my running clothes, and Mom and I went down to the track. There was a chill in the air, but it wasn't too cold—perfect weather for running. As we ran around and around in circles, I stopped feeling worried and sad and guilty.

It just goes to show you that sometimes it pays to listen to boring lectures in school!

CHAPTER 5

The War Begins

The second day of school was pretty good, especially since it was Friday, and there was a three-day weekend to look forward to. Two days of school, three days of break. Why can't it be like that year-round?

During lunch I tried not to think about Callie too much, but she and the PGC girls were making this big show of whispering and then looking over at us.

"That is *so* immature," Alexis said.

"Totally," Mia agreed. "It must have really upset them when we beat them last year."

"We should have another club meeting," I said. "We need to come up with something really amazing. Tonight we'll be busy baking for The Special

Day." Our friend Mona had a standing order with us, and we baked for her on Fridays.

"How about tomorrow afternoon?" Alexis suggested. "Mia and I have a soccer game in the morning, but we could do something around two."

"Sounds good," Emma said. "I have three dogs to walk in the morning, but I'm free in the afternoon."

"Hey, maybe I'll come watch your game," I said to Mia and Alexis. "I'll get my mom to drop me off."

"Then it's set," Alexis said. "We can meet at my house. Everyone should come with ideas."

I felt better knowing that we had a plan in place. I was not about to just sit back and let Callie beat us in a cupcake war!

The rest of the day was pretty good—until English class. Ms. Harmeyer asked everyone to hand in their poems. I had completely forgotten about it!

It is totally not like me to forget to do my homework. I got a sick feeling in my stomach. After class, I ran up to Ms. Harmeyer's desk.

"Ms. Harmeyer, I forgot to do my poem," I said. "I was waiting for my mom to help me and then things got . . . I just forgot. Can I do it over the weekend?"

Ms. Harmeyer shook her head. "I'm sorry, Katie. You're in middle school now, and my homework policy is very strict."

I felt like crying. "Okay," I said. "I won't forget again."

"I'll be offering an extra-credit assignment soon," she said.

I nodded. "Thanks," I said. "Have a nice weekend."

Things got much better once school was over. When I got off the bus, Mom was home, and she was cooking a Mexican-style chicken casserole—from scratch. Dinner was delicious, and at the end, Mom told me to close my eyes. When I opened them, she held out a plate with a perfect cupcake on it. The icing was blue, and there was a chocolate-covered graham cracker sticking up on top that looked like a chalkboard. A tiny white piece of candy next to the board looked like a piece of chalk. And Mom had written in icing on the board: "Back to School."

"I meant to make this for you on your first day, but I forgot," Mom said, and her eyes were a little teary. "I'm so sorry, Katie. I've got a lot on my mind lately."

"It's okay." I got up and gave her a hug. "This

is an awesome cupcake! I've got to take a picture."

I took out my cell phone, snapped a photo, and sent it to my friends.

Alexis replied first:

Nice! Good idea for contest maybe.

That reminded me. "Mom, can I go to a Cupcake Club meeting tomorrow? And there's a soccer game in the morning, too."

Mom nodded. "Sure. As long as your room is clean."

I could still close my closet door, so I knew I was okay.

"Yup," I answered.

The next morning was one of those hot September days that still feels like summer. By the time the soccer game was over, I was dripping with sweat—and I didn't even play! So I was glad we had our Cupcake Club meeting in Alexis's nice, air-conditioned kitchen.

When we arrived, Emma and her little brother, Jake, were already there. I happen to think that Jake is adorable, but I know he gets on Emma's nerves sometimes. Even though she has two older brothers, Emma gets stuck babysitting Jake a lot.

"Katie! Katie! I have a lizard!" Jake yelled, running toward me. He had something bright yellow and wiggly in his hand. For a second I thought it might be real, but when I got closer, I saw it was made of rubber. Still, I pretended to be scared.

"Oh no! A lizard!" I cried. "Is it slimy?"

"He's not slimy. His name is Charles," Jake said. "Here, feel him."

Jake put the rubber lizard in my hand. "He feels nice and smooth," I said.

Emma looked at me. "Sorry. Mom had to work the Saturday shift at the library."

"No problem," I said. I slid into my seat and pulled Jake onto my lap. "Jake can help us design our cupcakes. What kind of cupcakes should we make, Jake?"

"Lizard cupcakes!" he cried.

Mia laughed. "Now that's a winning idea."

"We need to get serious, guys," Alexis said. "We can't just *try* to win this fund-raiser. We *have* to win it *big-time*."

"Alexis is right," Emma agreed. "It would be terrible if the PGC beat us. It could really hurt our business."

Alexis flipped open her laptop. "I'll take notes,"

she said. "Katie, what do you know about Callie's baking skills?"

"She's pretty good," I admitted. "Her mom and my mom are friends, and they're the ones who taught me and Callie how to bake. I know Callie's mom will help her if she asks."

Alexis looked thoughtful. "I don't know about Maggie and Bella, but I'm pretty sure Bella doesn't bake. Vampires don't like to eat cupcakes, right?"

"I've heard Maggie say that her family goes out to restaurants all the time," Mia added. "So I bet Maggie doesn't know how to bake either."

"That definitely works in our favor," Alexis said, typing furiously. "We have a whole year of baking experience as a club."

"Hey, don't we have to register or something?" I remembered.

"I'll check the school's website," Alexis said, typing some more. After a few clicks, she stopped and raised her eyebrows. "Well, this is interesting."

I looked over her shoulder. "What?"

"There's a list of clubs that have entered already," Alexis said. "See this one? The BFC: the Best Friends Club. Callie Wilson, Maggie Rodriguez, and Bella Kovacs."

"They changed their name?" I asked.

43

"I don't get it," Alexis said, sitting back. "So what are they declaring? That they are now not popular?"

"Oh who cares?" I asked, suddenly feeling cranky. "I am so sick of them!"

Honestly, it felt like another direct blow from Callie. Like she was saying that Maggie and Bella were her best friends and not me. Which was true. But it felt personal. Like she was rubbing it in.

Alexis ignored my crankiness. "I mean, it makes no sense," she said. "Aren't they worried this will hurt their popularity? It seems risky."

"I don't know, it's kind of nice," Mia said. "When they called themselves the Popular Girls Club, it was obnoxious, right? But there's nothing obnoxious about being best friends."

Unless you dump your old best friend to get new ones, I thought. But I didn't say it.

"Maybe Callie is trying to make the PGC—I mean, the BFC—more friendly," Emma suggested.

"Whatever," I said. "Shouldn't we start planning our cupcakes?"

"Oh, before I forget, is everyone coming to our Labor Day barbecue on Monday?" Emma asked.

"Of course," Alexis replied.

"Me too," said Mia.

I cringed. I totally forgot to ask my mom about it. Every year we have this tradition of going to Callie's house on Labor Day. But being around Callie was the absolute last thing I wanted to do.

Mom will just have to understand, I thought. *I want to be with my* real *friends.*

"I still have to ask," I said. "So, anyway, we were talking about cupcakes. . . ."

"Lizard cupcakes!" Jake said, and everybody laughed.

CHAPTER 6

Think Fast, Katie!

When I got home from the Cupcake meeting, Mom was vacuuming the living room. I figured if I wanted to get out of Callie's barbecue, it wouldn't hurt to get on her good side, so I grabbed a broom and started sweeping the kitchen floor. Then I emptied the dishwasher.

"Thank you, Katie," Mom said, giving me a hug when I was done. "How was your Cupcake meeting?"

"It was good," I said. "Emma reminded me of something. She invited all of us to her house for a Labor Day barbecue on Monday."

"Labor Day!" Mom smacked her forehead with her palm. "Things have been so crazy that I never told Barbara if we were coming to the Wilsons' barbecue or not." (Barbara is Callie's mom, and my mom's best friend.)

"Do we have to go there?" I asked. "I'd rather be with my friends."

Mom sat down and bit her bottom lip, which she always does when she's worried or thinking.

"I need to get some shopping done for Grandma Carole's hospital stay, and I was hoping to cook some food and freeze it, so she won't have to cook while she's recovering," she said. "I suppose I could drop you off at Emma's while I get things done. I'm sure Barbara will understand."

"That would be great!" I said. "And I'll help you cook for Grandma and Grandpa if you want."

Mom smiled. "That would be fun. We can make a dish for you to bring to the barbecue, too."

So on Sunday we ended up cooking together, which was fun. I wanted to make an enchilada casserole for Grandma Carole, but Mom thought it might be too spicy for her. So instead we made a big pot of chicken soup. There was enough for us to have for dinner, with grilled cheese sandwiches on the side. *Yum!*

"We still need to make something for your barbecue," Mom said. "How about a pasta salad?"

"How about a *Mexican* pasta salad?" I suggested. (Can you tell yet that I am on a Mexican-food kick?)

"That sounds interesting," Mom said. "How would you do that?"

I thought about all of my favorite Mexican ingredients that we used in my cooking class. "I could put in black beans and tomatoes, and maybe some shredded cheese and some corn even. And avocados, of course!"

Mom nodded. "That sounds good. And you could put lime juice in the dressing. That could be tasty."

Because we've been cooking a lot of Mexican food, we had everything we needed in the house. Mom helped me cook the pasta—I used one of those squiggly shapes—and then when it cooled down, I mixed everything except the avocados together. I kept adding stuff and tasting it, and it was pretty good. Mom told me to wait to add the avocados until tomorrow, or else they would get brown.

So the next day at noon I was sitting in Mom's car with the bowl of Mexican pasta salad in my lap. When we pulled up we could already see a bunch of people at Emma's house. Her two older brothers,

Matt and Sam, were playing basketball in the driveway with a couple of their friends.

Both of Emma's brothers are nice. Matt is one grade above us, and he likes to tease all of us Cupcake Club members a lot. Sam is in high school, and he never teases us like Matt does. And even though they both have blond hair and blue eyes (just like Emma and Jake), I think Sam is cuter.

"I'll come get you around four," Mom said, leaning over to give me a kiss. "Have a good time. Call me on my cell if you need me, okay?"

"Sure, Mom," I said. Then I got out of the car, balancing the bowl as I tried to close the door.

"Think fast, Katie!"

A basketball whizzed past my face, and I looked up to see Matt grinning in the driveway. Sam ran to retrieve the ball as it bounced down the sidewalk.

"My hands are kind of full here!" I told Matt.

"Sorry," Matt said sheepishly. "I didn't know."

Sam ran up to me and tossed the ball to Matt. Then he peered into the plastic wrap–covered bowl.

"What is that?" he asked. "It looks good."

"It's, um, Katie's Mexican Special Salad," I said. "I just invented it."

"Well, if you made it, then it must be good," Sam said, and I could feel my face getting hot.

"I'd better bring it over to your mom," I said, and then quickly walked away.

I found Emma, Mia, and Alexis in the kitchen.

"Yay! Katie's here!" Emma said.

I held out the bowl. "I brought a Mexican pasta salad."

"Thanks," Emma said. "Let's bring it outside."

Emma's family has a big backyard, which is perfect for them, because they all like to play sports. The Taylors had set up a canopy for the party, and I put my pasta salad on a big picnic table that was covered with a blue flowered tablecloth. There was lots of food on the table already—pickles, green salad, cut-up veggies, potato salad, deviled eggs, and a plain pasta salad. I was glad I had made my pasta salad a little different.

Outside the canopy, Mr. Taylor, Emma's dad, was grilling chicken. On the grassy lawn beyond, Mrs. Taylor and some other adults were sitting in lawn chairs and talking.

Jake hurried over to us and shoved a Wiffle ball bat into my hands. "Katie, play baseball with me!"

There was no way I could disappoint a cute kid like Jake. Emma, Jake, and I decided to be on one team, and Mia and Alexis were on the other. We didn't play for real. We mostly just pitched the ball to one another and ran around.

Then all the boys came into the backyard.

"We want food!" Matt yelled.

"Matthew, whatever happened to 'please'?" called back Mrs. Taylor.

"Please!" Matthew said. "Give me some food!"

Mr. Taylor carried a big platter of barbecued chicken to the table. "No pushing, people. There's enough for everybody."

Emma rolled her eyes. "We'd better get over there if we want to eat. When there's food around, my brothers act like a school of angry piranhas."

"Don't call me a piranha!" Jake said. He looked mad.

Emma hugged him. "Not you, Jakey. *Those* two."

We walked over to the picnic table, and we could see that Emma was not exaggerating. The boys were piling their plates with humongous mountains of food. Sam was spooning my Mexican pasta salad onto his plate.

"Dude, save some for the rest of us!" Matt complained.

"Maybe," Sam said. "It's too good."

Then Matt punched Sam in the arm, and Sam almost dropped his plate. Luckily, Mrs. Taylor appeared just in time.

"All right, boys, that's enough," she said. "We've got hot dogs coming up next if you're still hungry."

There was still plenty of food left, so the Cupcakers got our plates together and then went to sit on a blanket Emma had spread out for us under one of the trees in her yard. For a minute, I couldn't help but think of all my past Labor Days, which I spent hanging out with Callie at her house. It was a little weird to be somewhere new, but I had my three best friends with me. And that felt good.

Even better, we didn't talk about Callie or the BFC or even the fund-raiser. We talked about teachers and that new cooking contest reality show on TV, and Alexis complained about her older sister, Dylan, and Mia complained about her stepbrother, Dan.

"My grandma Carole's going to have heart surgery," I blurted out during the conversation. I'm not sure why I said it, but I guess I wanted my friends to know.

"Oh no! Is she going to be okay?" Emma said.

"My mom says she will be," I answered.

"Your grandma is supernice," Alexis said. "Maybe we should make her some get-well cupcakes. Free of charge, of course."

I smiled. Alexis may be all about business some-times, but she has a big heart, too.

"I hope everything goes okay, Katie," Mia said. "I'm going to make your grandma a get-well card."

"You guys are the best," I said, and I meant it. Then I leaned back on the blanket and looked up at the blue sky that peeked through the leaves of the tree. For that moment, everything was perfect.

I really like it when that happens.

CHAPTER 7

I Can't Believe She Did That!

The next day we had school again, and now that Labor Day was over, it felt more real. Like summer was definitely over, even if it was still kind of hot out.

The teachers were taking it seriously too, and on Tuesday, I got slammed with homework in every class. I didn't want to mess up like I had with my English homework last week, so I made sure to write down everything in my assignment book.

Something else happened on Tuesday too. That's when Callie started acting totally different. Well, not *totally* different, but she wasn't acting like the Callie I knew. The BFC Callie was acting even worse than the PGC Callie.

Let me give you some examples. On Tuesday the Cupcake Club was eating lunch when Sophie and Lucy came over to our table. They're mostly friends with Mia, but they're nice to everyone.

"Congratulations, Mia, you made the list," Sophie said. But she didn't say it in an excited way. She sounded more sarcastic.

"What list?" Mia asked.

Lucy nodded over to the BFC table. "Callie, Maggie, and Bella invited us to eat lunch with them today. So we said yes, and while we were there, they started making a list of who has the best hair today and who has lame hair. Can you believe it?"

"That is so rude," Alexis exclaimed, fuming.

"Yeah, you and Katie are both on the lame-hair list," Sophie told us.

That made me mad, but I decided to make a joke about it instead.

"Oh no! I guess my dreams of being a famous hair model are over," I said, and everyone laughed.

Alexis stood up. "I should go over there and tear that list to pieces."

"Don't do it," Mia said. "We can't show them that it bothers us."

"Why should it bother you? You're on the good list," Alexis said.

"It bothers me because you guys are my friends," Mia said.

"I must be invisible," Emma said, twirling a strand of her blond hair. "I'm not even on the list at all. I think that's even more insulting."

"Just thought you should know," Sophie said with a shrug, and the two girls walked off.

Alexis didn't look mad anymore. She looked thoughtful. "Interesting," she said. "I wonder why they invited Sophie and Lucy to sit with them."

"Maybe they're recruiting new members," Emma suggested.

"They probably just want to find somebody to make their cupcakes for them, so they don't have to do the dirty work," I said, feeling cranky again.

"I don't know," Mia said. "The PGC was always so closed off. Maybe Callie is trying to open things up and be a little friendlier."

Alexis snorted. "Right. The 'new and improved' BFC led by the 'new and improved' Callie."

So the hair thing is one example. Then there's the whole flirting thing. In social studies, Callie and Maggie were whispering to each other before the bell rang. Then Tyler Norstrom, this tall boy on the basketball team, walked into the room. When he walked past Callie's desk, I noticed she did this thing where she tossed her hair over her shoulder. Then she looked straight at Tyler and batted her eyelashes at him.

You know, Callie is really pretty, and I guess she can pull off that kind of stuff if she wants to. But this hair-tossing person was not the Callie I grew up with. Now she was becoming more like Sydney every day.

After school on Tuesday, I went right home and started on my mountain of homework. I decided to do my English first, so I wouldn't forget it. I scanned the instruction sheet. We had to write about the assigned book we read over the summer. There were all these choices on what to write, and I picked writing a letter about the book. I wrote a really good letter, giving all the details of the book, and it was one page longer than Ms. Harmeyer asked for. I was pretty satisfied when I was done, because I knew it would impress her.

The next morning I saw Callie in the hallway. She was at her locker with Maggie and Bella. Then my friend Beth Suzuki from Spanish class walked by. Beth has a kind of funky fashion style, like Mia. She was wearing black leggings and a black top, with a black-and-white scarf around her neck and red high-tops.

I actually heard Callie say, "Red sneakers?

Seriously?" It wasn't a particularly funny or clever thing to say, but both Bella and Maggie laughed. I don't think Beth heard them, though.

And those examples aren't even the worst. At lunchtime, I was in the hall, walking to the cafeteria, when Callie came over to me.

"Hey, Katie," she said. "Do you want to eat lunch with us today?"

I felt like a bus hit me. What was Callie up to? I was really surprised. Then I realized she was waiting for an answer. Well, whatever her plans were, I wasn't about to give her any satisfaction.

"No, thanks," I said. "I always sit with my *friends*."

Callie flinched, like she was shocked by my answer. "What gives?" she asked me. "I'm trying to be nice here."

"You mean nice, like when you put me on your lame-hair list?" I asked.

Callie's face turned a little red. "Maggie did that."

"Right. Because *her* hair is so awesome," I said. I knew that was childish, but I couldn't help it.

"We were just goofing around," Callie said. "Come on, sit with us."

On a scale of one to ten, my annoyance level with Callie was at a hundred.

"If you're trying to make things up to me, it's a little late," I said. "And don't expect me to jump when you ask me to do stuff, like Bella and Maggie do."

"Wow, and I thought you were my friend," Callie said, acting hurt.

"I *was* your friend. Your best friend," I replied. "And then you dumped me for Sydney. You let Sydney say mean stuff about me, and you didn't stick up for me. Half the time you acted like you didn't know me. So don't tell *me* I'm not a good friend. I never did anything like that to you."

I could feel my eyes stinging, and I saw a few people staring at us as they walked by.

Do not cry, I warned myself. *You will never live it down.*

"You—you don't know how much pressure I'm under," Callie stammered. "I just wanted to be popular. . . . When Sydney asked me to join the PGC last year, I couldn't say no. I asked her to stop teasing you in gym class, but she wouldn't listen."

"Then you should have stopped being friends with her," I said flatly. "I wouldn't be friends with somebody who was mean to you."

Callie shook her head. "You don't understand.

It wasn't that simple. But Sydney's gone now, anyway. So I thought—"

"Sorry, Callie," I interrupted. "My friends are waiting for me."

I turned and walked into the noisy cafeteria. My heart was pounding really fast. I felt hurt and sad and mad and good, all at the same time.

I had wanted to say that stuff to Callie for months.

CHAPTER 8

A Totally Groovy Theme

At lunch, I didn't tell my friends what happened, because I was feeling kind of rattled. But I was in the mood to talk about it that night, when Mom and I were eating Chinese take-out. And yes, if you're counting, that's take-out again. What can I say, Mom was on a roll? But I love Chinese food, so I wasn't complaining.

"So, Mom," I said, twirling a lo mein on my plate. "Something weird happened in school today. Callie asked me to eat lunch at her table!"

"That's nice, honey," Mom said.

"No, it is *not* nice!" I insisted. "You know Callie has been ignoring me for a year so she can hang out with girls who are mean to me. And just because Sydney's gone, she thinks I'll just run over and sit with her. Can you believe that?"

While I was talking, Mom was texting someone on her cell phone.

"Mom! Are you listening?" I asked.

Mom put down the phone. "It sounds like she's trying to make things up to you. I'm not sure why you're so upset."

"Forget it," I said, and Mom picked up her phone again. Now I was upset about Callie *and* Mom. Why was everyone acting so weird?

On Thursday night we had a Cupcake Club meeting at Mia's house. Mia wasn't going to be around for the weekend, because she stays with her dad in New York City every other weekend. Her parents are divorced, like mine, only I don't get to see my dad. I think Mia's pretty lucky, even though she has to sort of live in two different places. But she doesn't seem to mind.

Anyway, Mia's house is fun, because she has two little fluffy dogs, Milkshake and Tiki. Plus, Mia's mom and her stepdad, Eddie, let us have a dinner meeting.

We ate pizza (with no veggies!) in the dining room as we tried—once again—to come up with plans for the school fund-raiser. But first I was finally ready to tell my friends about my face-off with Callie.

"No way!" Alexis said when I was done with the story. "Who does she think she is?"

"It's kind of weird she doesn't realize how much she hurt your feelings before," Emma said.

"I know, right?" I said. It felt good to have my friends back me up.

"I don't know," Mia said cautiously. "I mean, it sounds like she tried to make up with you."

"She probably just wants to convert Katie to the BFC, so that she can bake the cupcakes," Alexis said.

I hadn't thought of that. But it was possible that Alexis was on to something.

"Well, that will *never* happen," I promised. "Cupcake Club forever!"

Alexis opened up her laptop. "Well, there might not *be* a Cupcake Club if we lose the fund-raiser," she said dramatically.

"Hey, Alexis, what happened to your notebook?" I asked.

"In the Future Business Leaders of America we're encouraged to use our laptops," she said. "It's more efficient."

"Maybe we could google some cupcake ideas," Mia suggested.

"I like that back-to-school cupcake that Katie's mom made her"—Alexis flipped the laptop around to show the photo that I sent everyone—"but we might need to charge a lot for it to cover our overall production costs."

"Let's start with a design," Mia suggested. "Then we can pick a flavor that goes with the design."

"We have to think of something everybody likes," I said. "What about the beach? Everyone likes the beach, right? Maybe we can do a tropical cupcake, and we can decorate the booth with beach balls and stuff."

"That's fun, but it doesn't feel like school, or fall," Mia pointed out.

I sighed. "I know."

Alexis was furiously surfing the Web. "You know, it's the fiftieth anniversary of Park Street Middle School this year. Maybe we could do something with that."

"Like cupcakes with a big 'fifty' on them?" Emma asked.

Alexis thought for a moment. "Hmm . . . so the school opened in the 1960s. Maybe we could do a sixties theme."

"Like a groovy peace-and-love kind of theme?" I asked.

"That would be so cool," Mia agreed. "We could do tie-dyed icing! And T-shirts to match!"

"And we could decorate the cupcakes with peace signs," Emma added.

I really loved the idea. Anytime I get to wear rainbow colors, I'm happy.

"If we do tie-dyed icing, we should keep the flavors simple," Alexis said. "Chocolate or vanilla. Most people like simple flavors, anyway."

"How do we make tie-dyed icing?" Emma asked.

Mia shrugged. "I'm not sure. But I bet we could figure it out."

"I'll see if there's anything online," Alexis said, and started typing.

"Mia, do you think your mom would mind if we baked?" I asked.

Mia shook her head. "Nope. She even bought extra eggs and milk, just in case we wanted to."

"Then let's clean up the pizza and get started," I said. "I have an idea."

By now I think the Cupcake Club has baked thousands of cupcakes. Okay, maybe not thousands, but at least hundreds. So we can whip up a dozen vanilla cupcakes in no time.

After about a half hour we had a pan of cupcakes

baking in the oven. Mia's stepdad, Eddie, came into the room and smelled the air.

"Mmm, I love when you girls have Cupcake meetings at this house," he said.

"This is just a test batch, so you'll definitely get some," Mia promised him.

Eddie smiled. "It's my lucky day!"

While the cupcakes baked, we mixed powdered sugar, butter, a little milk, and some vanilla together to make a basic vanilla frosting.

"Mia, do you have food coloring?" I asked.

"Sure." Mia went to the cabinet and came back with a package that contained five little bottles of liquid food coloring. First, I put in a few drops of yellow. Then I swirled it around with the tip of my knife.

"Ooh, pretty," Emma said. "Can I try?"

I nodded, and Emma put in some blue and then swirled it around the yellow. Then Mia did the same thing with red, and Alexis added green.

"It looks pretty good," I said. "Now we just have to see how it looks on the cupcakes."

After the cupcakes were done baking and we'd let them cool, we tried spreading the tie-dyed icing on them. But when we did that, the colors started blending together, and the color ended up looking like a depressing purplish brown.

I frowned. "Sorry, guys."

"No, we almost had it," Mia said. "I think it'll work if we ice the cupcakes *first*, and then do the swirly food-coloring thing."

Emma frowned. "That will take forever, won't it?"

"It might, but we want to win, don't we?" Alexis pointed out.

"It won't be so bad," I said. "Besides, I think if we use the gel food coloring, the color will be easier to control."

Eddie came back into the kitchen and made a face. "What kind of icing is that?"

"Ugly but delicious," I told him.

Mia handed him one. "You can taste test it for us. I know you love to do that."

Eddie peeled away the cupcake liner and took a bite. "It *is* delicious!" he said. "But I need some milk."

Eddie took five cups out of the cabinet, got the milk out of the refrigerator, and put everything on the table. "Won't you ladies join me?"

We all sat down. Mia poured the milk, and we all happily ate our cupcakes and drank our milk.

"There's nothing like cake and milk," Eddie said. "It reminds me of being a little boy."

"Eddie, you were a little boy in the sixties, right?" Alexis asked.

Eddie nodded. "That's right. Why do you ask?"

"I've got an idea," Mia said. "We could sell milk to go with our cupcakes, just like in the old days."

"Old days? Hey, I'm not that old," Eddie protested.

"You know, my mom and I get our milk from this place that sells it in old-fashioned glass bottles," I said. "We could pour the milk from those and then recycle the empty bottles. We can donate that money to the school too."

Eddie nodded. "It sounds like you girls have a good idea."

I grinned and made a peace sign with my fingers. "It's not just good. It's totally groovy!"

CHAPTER 9

Ugh! Another Poem

The next day was Cupcake Friday. We started calling it that because that's the day one of us brings in cupcakes for lunch. This week it was Mia's turn.

"Ta-da!" she said, opening up the small box she had brought. Inside were four perfect cupcakes. The icing on top was light blue and green, and it was piped on, so that it looked like ocean waves, or feathers, even.

"They are so pretty," I said.

"They're plain vanilla, but I'm practicing with those new decorating tips I got," Mia said. "Once you get the hang of it, it's easy."

"If you put candy fish on top, it could look like the ocean," Emma suggested.

"We need to keep a database of these ideas,"

Alexis said. "Maybe someone will ask us to do a pool party or something. These would be perfect. We just have to remember."

"I have a file of stuff at home," I said. "It's full of recipes and pictures of cupcakes from magazines."

Alexis nodded. "We should scan all that in onto my laptop. Maybe we could do it this weekend?"

I shook my head. "We're spending the weekend at my grandma's," I said. Mom had told me last night.

"Oh, that reminds me," Mia said. "I made a card for her."

Mia dug into her backpack and pulled out a card made of folded scrapbook paper. On the front she had drawn a robin, Grandma Carole's favorite bird, and surrounded it with lots of flowers.

"I remembered the robin from when we made that birthday cupcake cake for her," Mia said.

"Mia, it's so beautiful!" I said. "She'll love it."

"Katie, Emma and I were going to make a card for her this weekend," Alexis said.

"You guys can sign this one," Mia offered.

Everyone signed the card. Then I put it away, so it wouldn't get cupcake icing on it.

"Oh, by the way," Alexis said. "In French class

today, Maggie and Bella were whispering really loudly about the BFC cupcakes. They kept saying it was a huge secret and everyone was going to be blown away."

"They can try," I said. "But our cupcakes are going to be awesome."

The rest of the afternoon went pretty slowly, probably because it was Friday and I couldn't wait for school to be over. The last class of the day was English, and at the start of class, Ms. Harmeyer handed back our homework from earlier in the week. I was excited, because I knew I did really well on the assignment.

So you can imagine how I felt when I got my paper back and saw a big red C on it. I was totally shocked. I was dying to ask Ms. Harmeyer about it, and it was torture to wait until the end of class. When the bell rang, I ran up to her desk.

"Ms. Harmeyer, um, I have a question," I said. "I thought I did a really good job on this. I even wrote extra. So . . ."

"It was very well written, Katie," Ms. Harmeyer said. "But you didn't follow the instructions. You were supposed to write the letter from the point of view of one of the characters in the book. So I had to lower your grade because of that."

I couldn't believe it. I was sure I had done everything just right! My eyes got hot. What was up with me lately? Everything was making me want to cry.

Ms. Harmeyer lost the serious expression she usually wore. "Katie, I understand you did exceptionally well in English last year," she said. "But you seem to be struggling so far this year. Is everything all right?"

"I guess," I said. "I mean, my grandma needs to have an operation, and my mom's really worried, and then there's this whole thing going on with this girl I used to be friends with. . . ."

Ms. Harmeyer nodded. "I thought it might be something like that. I do think you need to focus more on your schoolwork if you can, Katie. But I'll give you a special extra-credit assignment, okay?"

"Really?" I asked. "Thank you sooo much!"

"I'll make it easy," she said. "Write me a poem. It can be about anything you want. It's due next Thursday."

I made a face. "A poem?"

"What's the matter?" the teacher asked. "Don't you like poetry?"

"It's okay," I said. "But it's hard to write. It's like I know what I want to say, but then I can't make it rhyme or put the right number of beats on each line. So it comes out all wrong."

"Not all poetry has to rhyme," Ms. Harmeyer told me. "I'll tell you what. You spend the weekend thinking of what you want your poem to be about. On Monday I'll bring in some examples of different types of poetry, and we can look at them together. Then maybe you'll feel better about poems."

"Okay," I said, nodding. "Thanks."

I dreaded showing Mom the C I got on my homework, but when she saw it that night, she said basically the same thing as Ms. Harmeyer.

"I know you have a lot on your mind, Katie," Mom said. "I'm sorry if I haven't been acting like myself lately. I'm sure it will all calm down after Grandma's surgery. Can you hang in there for me?"

"Don't worry, Mom. It's okay," I said. "Plus, Ms. Harmeyer gave me an extra-credit assignment, so I can make up the grade."

That night, we packed our bags, and the next morning we headed out to Grandma Carole and Grandpa Chuck's house. We live in the same state, but they live near the ocean, in one of those places where the houses are all owned by old people— or senior citizens, as my mom always tells me to say. (For some reason, old people do not like to be called old.)

On the ride down we listened to the radio, and I stared out the window at the trees. I tried to think of an idea for my poem. I could write about cupcakes. Or maybe I could write a poem about how awesome my grandma Carole is. That would be nice.

Suddenly, as I was thinking about Grandma Carole, I got sad. What if this was the last time I got to see her, ever? Mom said she was going to be okay. I had to believe that.

When we finally got to Grandma and Grandpa's little yellow house, Grandma Carole was standing by the open front door with a big smile on her face. I totally stopped worrying. She looked just like she always does. Her white hair was cut short, and she wore a blue T-shirt with white exercise pants, and sneakers.

"I'm so lucky! I get both of my girls this weekend!" Grandma said, hugging us.

"How are you feeling?" I asked her.

"Not bad, Katie, not bad," Grandma said. "I'll feel better when the surgery is over with. But between my doctors and Grandpa Chuck and your mom, I'm in very good hands."

"Hey, I need some hugs too!" Grandpa Chuck called out. He was in the living room, his feet resting on an ottoman.

"Hope you don't mind if I don't get up," he said as I bent down to hug him. "Doctor says I need one of those new-fangled bionic knees. But that won't happen until your grandma is back on her feet."

"That won't take long at all," Grandma promised.

"Grandma, I have something for you," I said. I reached into my overnight bag and got out the get-well card that Mia had made and we all signed.

"Oh, how beautiful!" Grandma said, and her eyes got teary (maybe that's where I get it from).

Normally, when we visit my grandparents, we go out and do stuff. We drive to the beach and then walk around, or play tennis, or go to the driving range to hit golf balls. But I guess Grandma wasn't supposed to do that stuff, because all morning, Mom and Grandma Carole were doing paperwork, and Grandpa Chuck and I were watching TV. It was kind of boring.

Then I helped Mom make lunch, and I got an idea.

"Mom, do you think Grandma would make cupcakes with us?" I asked. "Maybe we could bring them to the nurses at her doctor's office."

"That's a lovely idea," Mom said. "But we've got to do all the dishes, okay?"

"Of course!" I said.

So for the rest of the afternoon we looked through Grandma's old recipe book and picked out a recipe for banana cinnamon cupcakes. Then we made them, and Grandpa Chuck put on his favorite country music CD. We sang and joked around, and I didn't worry about Grandma Carole one bit.

That's the good thing about making cupcakes. While you're doing it, it's hard to worry about other stuff. And at the end you get something delicious to eat. Maybe if everyone baked more cupcakes, the world would be a happier place.

CHAPTER 10

A Bad Day

$\mathcal{I}$ ended up having fun visiting Grandma Carole and Grandpa Chuck, but I was glad when we got home on Sunday. I had lots of homework to do, and by Monday morning I was really eager to see my friends.

Since I knew I had to focus on work, I decided I had to ignore Callie as much as possible. Mostly, it was easy to do because Callie didn't seem interested in talking to me (or even looking at me), either. Sometimes it was harder to do, especially because we had a few classes together. But Mia being in the same classes too made it okay.

Then, when I needed her most, Mia had to leave school, because she had a bad toothache. She left in the middle of social studies. I felt bad for her, but since Mia's dentist is my mom, I knew she would be okay.

The next class was science with Ms. Chandar. That day, we were doing a lab where we had to mix some chemicals together in a beaker and then watch the reaction. Normally I'm pretty good at this kind of thing, because it's sort of like baking. Plus, with Mia as my lab partner, it would've been easy.

But without Mia, I was on my own.

"It is a simple experiment, Katie," Ms. Chandar said. "You can do it without a partner."

We went to get our ingredients for the experiment, which was a container of blue stuff and a container of clear stuff. I listened carefully as Ms. Chandar told us how to measure out the blue stuff and then pour it into the clear stuff. I carefully began to pour—and then I sneezed.

I don't know where it came from. It was one of those random sneezes. It took me by surprise, and I dropped the beaker. The blue stuff spilled all over the lab table in front of me.

Ms. Chandar didn't notice, so I had to raise my hand.

"I had an accident," I told her, which is a pretty embarrassing thing to have to say in front of the whole class.

Ms. Chandar sighed. "The towels are in the cabinet at the back of the room."

As I headed for the towels, I noticed that my hands were bright blue. And, of course, I had to walk right past Maggie and Bella's table to get to the towels.

"Way to go, Katie," Maggie said, giggling.

"Is that how you make your cupcakes, too?" Bella asked.

I ignored them and got the towels. Then I had to walk past them again.

"Look! Katie has Smurf hands!" Maggie said, and now a bunch of kids were laughing.

"She's Clumsy Smurf!" Bella said, and then they both started cracking up.

My face turned red, but I just kept walking. You won't believe what happened next. Eddie Rossi walked up to Maggie and Bella.

"Cut it out, guys," he said. "It was just an accident."

Maggie and Bella quickly stopped laughing. I know they think Eddie is cute, and they both looked kind of embarrassed.

Thank you, I mouthed to Eddie, and then hurried to my desk and started wiping up the mess.

Weird, right? I mean, normally Eddie would have started cracking up too and calling me Smurf Face or something.

Maybe Alexis and Mia are right, I thought. *Maybe he does like me.*

Which was even weirder, because, well, I don't think of Eddie like that. But it was definitely interesting.

When I got home from school, I wanted to talk to Mia about it, but I didn't want to bug her if her tooth was still hurting her.

When Mom came home from work, the first thing I asked was "How's Mia?"

"She's got a cavity, but she's feeling better already," Mom said. "I'm seeing her again tomorrow after school, to go over her X-rays. One of her permanent teeth is growing in a little bit strange."

"I'm glad she's okay," I said. I took out my cell phone to text her, but then Mom kept talking.

"Katie, I need to discuss something with you," Mom said. "Mrs. Rogers's daughter's baby came early, so she can't come stay with you this weekend."

"Hooray!" I said. "So I can stay at Mia's, right?"

Mom shook her head. "Just on Friday night, when you're making cupcakes. But you'll be going home with the Wilsons after the fund-raiser. I won't be home until late Tuesday, and I want to make sure you're in good hands while I'm gone."

I was completely shocked. "No way!" I protested. "You can't expect me to go over to Callie's! She's, like, my mortal enemy now!"

Mom sighed. "Katie, it's decided. This is not up for discussion."

"But it's not fair!" I yelled, and I was definitely crying now. "I can't stand being around Callie! Why can't I just stay at Mia's the whole time?"

"Because it's a lot to ask for you to stay with someone for that long. Barbara is my best friend, and I don't want to have to worry about you while I'm worried about Grandma and everything else," Mom said in a rush. "End of story."

"You don't understand!" I wailed. "You can't do this to me!"

"Katie, enough!" Mom yelled, which is something she almost never does. "I know you've been having problems with Callie for a while now, but Grandma Carole is a lot more important than your silly dramas with your friends. You're going to stay at Callie's, and you're just going to have to deal with it. Now go to your room until you cool off."

I ran out of the living room and stomped up the stairs as hard and as loud as I could. Then I went into my room, slammed the door behind me, and fell facedown onto my bed.

I cried for a while, and then I texted Mia.

Mom says I have 2 stay with Callie for 4 days while she is gone! How am I supposed to do that?

I'll ask my mom if you can stay here, Mia texted.
It's no use. She's best friends with Callie's mom, so she doesn't care that Callie and I are enemies now, I typed.
Maybe it won't be so bad, Mia said.
I don't even want to breathe the same air as her, I wrote back.

The next message I got from Mia was a photo of an astronaut.

U can wear this, she wrote.
LOL, I typed, and I really was.

Mia can always make me feel better. Then I remembered—Mia needed to feel better too.

How is your tooth? I asked.

Better, she replied. Ur Mom is nice.

Aaaaaa! Only sometimes! I wrote.

Now, I know that wasn't exactly true. She is nice most of the time. But right then I was superangry with her.

After I said good-bye to Mia, I went to my desk and turned on my laptop. I knew exactly what my poem was going to be about.

CHAPTER 11

Now I'm Confused Again

There is a black cloud in my heart.
When it rains, I cry.
Nothing is fair.
Nothing is fair.
Why do people get sick?
Why do friends fight?

I won't write the whole poem here now, because it's kind of long, but you get the idea. Once I realized I didn't have to rhyme, then it was kind of easy. I just concentrated on my feelings. Plus, I made sure to put in some metaphors and similes, to make Ms. Harmeyer happy, so I could get a good grade.

I have to admit that I actually felt better after I wrote the poem. Kind of like my angry feelings left me and attached to the paper or something. Running makes me feel better too, but in a different way. When I run, worries and other feelings leave my body, but I guess with poetry, those feelings float away into the air.

The next day, it was hard to even look at Callie, though, because my stomach flip-flopped every time I thought about having to stay with her. Thank goodness for my friends. At least they understood.

"That's just awful!" Emma said when I told her and Alexis about it during lunch. Mia sat next to me and nodded sympathetically.

"You could stay at my house," Alexis offered.

"Or mine," Emma added.

I shook my head. "Thanks, but I already tried seeing if I could stay at Mia's. Mom's being totally unfair about it."

"It'll go by fast," Mia said.

"Bring headphones with you," Alexis suggested.

I sighed. "I'll just be glad when this is over."

"Hey, Mom said we could do the test batch at our house tonight," Emma said. "Is seven okay?"

Everyone said that would be fine.

"Mom and I bought the ingredients over the weekend," Emma continued.

"I hope you saved your receipt," said Alexis.

Emma rolled her eyes. "Of course! I know you would never let me forget it if I didn't."

I suddenly felt nervous. "It feels like we still have a ton of things to do," I said. "What about the decorations and everything?"

"I made a tie-dyed tablecloth for us at Dad's last weekend," Mia reported. "Ava helped me."

"And my dad's going to get the milk for us on Saturday morning," Alexis said. "He's going to donate the milk, since it's for a good cause."

"Oh, and we found the cutest striped straws to put in the cups of milk!" Emma reported. "They're rainbow colored, to go with the tie-dyed theme."

"And we're going to wear aprons that we can decorate with peace symbols and stuff," Alexis said.

"Wow," I said. "You guys did all that?"

"We were texting all weekend," Alexis said. "We didn't want to bother you at your grandma's."

For a second I didn't know if my feelings should be hurt, but then I decided they shouldn't be. I'm glad I spent the weekend with Grandma Carole instead of worrying about the fund-raiser.

"Thanks for doing all that," I said.

"Besides, Katie, we're counting on you to make the cupcakes as groovy as possible," Mia added.

I nodded. "I'll feel better after we do the test batch."

Mia frowned. "I've got to go back to your mom after school today. I hope I can still get my homework done, or I might not be able to come."

"Don't worry about it," Alexis said. "It's just a test. Friday night is when we'll need all four of us to really work."

I made a fake-sad face. "Now I have to ride the bus by myself again!"

"Well, at least you won't have metal tools in your mouth," Mia said.

"Good point," I agreed.

I still had four classes to go before the bus, and at least I had Mia with me for social studies and science. When we got to science class, I whispered the story of what had happened with Eddie the day before. Mia nodded.

"I *told* you he likes you!" she whispered back.

I shook my head. I still couldn't believe it.

Then in drama class we learned some interesting stuff about the history of theater in ancient Greece, and in English class I handed in my poem to Ms. Harmeyer. This time, I was *sure* I had done a good job. I couldn't wait to get it back.

When school was out, I slid into my usual seat

on the bus: the sixth row from the front. Then something very surprising happened. George Martinez sat next to me!

"Hey," he said.

"Hey," I said back. I felt a little nervous all of a sudden. What could George want?

"So, with that social studies homework, are we supposed to answer all those review questions or just the fill-in ones at the top?" he asked.

All right, I thought. *He's just asking about homework. That's cool.*

I took out my assignment book and looked through it. "All of them," I told him.

George sighed. "Man, I hate those questions on the bottom. They take so long to do."

"I know," I agreed. "Do you think Mrs. Kratzer even reads all those answers?"

"I bet she does," George says. "She looks like she loves to read. I bet her house is full of books."

"Just because she wears glasses?" I asked.

George shrugged. "I don't know. It's just . . . that's how she looks."

That reminded me of something. "We were watching this old TV show at my grandparents' house, and there was this episode where this guy loved books, and then the world ended or something. But he was happy, because he could read all the time. And then his eyeglasses broke!"

"*The Twilight Zone,*" George said. "My dad loves that show. He has them all on DVD. That was a good episode."

I shuddered. "That show is supercreepy. I'd rather see a funny show."

"Did you see that new cartoon about the chicken that's trying to rule the world?" George asked.

I nodded. (Yes, I still watch cartoons sometimes.) "That show is hysterical. Like when he tried to attack the city with that giant omelet?"

"'More onions! More onions!'" George yelled, imitating the chicken, and we both started cracking up.

Then I realized something. George and I were having an actual conversation, just like I would have with Mia or Alexis or Emma. We weren't just goofing around or teasing each other. It was kind of nice.

I was laughing so hard that I almost missed getting off at my bus stop.

"Hey, Katie!" the bus driver yelled. "You're up."

I grabbed my backpack. "See ya," I told George.

As the bus drove past, George waved to me

through the window. I couldn't help thinking about what Mia had said on the first day of school.

I think they both like you!

It was all so strange. I definitely didn't know how I felt about Eddie liking me, if he did. But when I thought about George liking me, I decided I didn't mind so much.

Aaaaah! My face was getting red just thinking about it.

CHAPTER 12

Spectacular!

*L*ater that night, Alexis, Emma, and I did a test batch of the cupcakes (Mia couldn't make it after all), and this time the icing came out perfectly. So when Friday rolled around, we were ready for a marathon baking session. First we'd bake our cupcakes for Mona and then work on our contest cupcakes.

My mom dropped me off at Mia's at four o'clock. Our car was packed with stuff: my sleeping bag; a big duffel bag full of my clothes; my school backpack; four cupcake pans; four cooling racks; a box of stuff for the booth; and a Crock-Pot filled with veggie chili and a basket of corn bread, because Mom felt bad that Mia's mom and stepdad had to feed us dinner again.

"You didn't have to do this, Sharon," Mrs. Valdes said as she and Mia helped us unload the car. "I know you've got so much to do these days."

"I don't mind," Mom said. "I wish I could help out more. Thanks so much for hosting the girls tonight and for letting Katie sleep over. Did you get the phone numbers I sent you?"

Mia's mom nodded. "We'll take good care of Katie, we promise. I hope everything works out all right with your mother."

Mom smiled. "Me too," she said with a sigh. "Thanks."

After we got everything into Mia's house, I walked with Mom back to the car.

"Now, don't forget. Mrs. Wilson is going to bring you home after the fund-raiser tomorrow," Mom reminded me.

"I know," I said glumly.

Mom hugged me. "I love you," she said. "Don't worry. Everything will be okay."

I knew Mom was talking about Grandma, and that made me feel good. But Mom still didn't really understand, or didn't really care, how I felt about staying with Callie. That definitely did *not* feel okay.

I went back inside, and Alexis and Emma

showed up a few minutes later. We all gathered in Mia's kitchen. It's nice and big, with an island in the middle, so it's a good space to make a ton of cupcakes.

"Okay, troops, it's time for battle!" Alexis announced. "We've got a lot to do if we're going to beat the BFC."

I saluted. "What's the plan, General?"

"First, we bake," Alexis said. "While the cupcakes bake, we'll make the icing. When the cupcakes cool, I was thinking you and Mia could ice them while Emma and I work on the aprons."

Emma held up a plain white apron. "I brought some fabric pens, so we can draw peace signs and stuff on them."

"Awesome," I said. "I'll start loading the cupcake tins."

Between the four of us, we had eight cupcake tins. I lined them up on Mia's kitchen table. Mia came over with a paper bag.

"Look what I found at that fancy bake shop," she said. She pulled out two packs of cupcake liners with a tie-dyed pattern.

"Oh my gosh, they're perfect!" I cried. "But wait a second. This is a fund-raiser, right? How are we paying for all this?"

"Well, my mom and dad donated the baking supplies," Emma said.

"And my dad's getting the milk," Alexis reminded them. "We'll have to pay for the aprons and cupcake liners out of our general fund. But I like to think of it as advertising. We could get a bunch of customers out of this." Then she frowned. "Rats! I made a flyer for us to hand out, but I forgot to print it. Let me text my mom."

Pretty soon we were in our usual cupcake-making groove. We made a batch of batter in Mia's stand mixer. We filled the tins. Then we made a new batch. We kept baking until we had two hundred and four cupcakes cooling on the table—that's seventeen dozen!

That's when Mia's mom came in. "I think it's time you girls had a break," she said. "Dinner's ready in the dining room."

We washed up and then headed into the dining room, where the table was set for seven: the Cupcake Club; Mrs. Valdes; Eddie; and Mia's stepbrother, Dan. Besides Mom's chili and corn bread, there was a big salad on the table.

"You girls are busy bees in there," Eddie said, and he started scooping the chili into bowls.

"We have sooo much left to do," I lamented.

"I think you girls are doing great," said Mia's mom. "It's not even seven o'clock yet."

"When do we get to taste them?" Eddie asked.

"Soon," Mia promised. "We already made one batch of icing. Then Katie's going to do her swirly tie-dyed magic on the cupcakes."

"It's easy," I said. "You'll be able to do it too."

Dan didn't say much—he never does. But maybe that's because he was busy eating. He ate three bowls of chili and four pieces of corn bread. I glanced at Mia after Dan went for his fourth bowl.

She shrugged. "He's working out a lot lately. Getting ready for basketball season."

Dan nodded. "Besides, this stuff is awesome."

Dan was still eating when we got up, cleared our plates, and got to work on icing the cupcakes. Mia put a smooth coat of vanilla icing on the first cupcake and then handed it to me.

I was armed with a box of toothpicks and several tubes of gel color. I put a tiny drop of yellow onto the icing and then swirled it with a toothpick. Then I swirled on a drop of green and then a drop of blue.

"Awesome!" Mia said. "That looks perfect!"

"See? You can so do it," I told her.

Mia nodded. "I'll ice and you swirl, and then we'll switch."

Mia and I got busy with the icing, and once the dining room table was clear, Alexis and Emma used it as their work space to do the aprons. We had four dozen cupcakes done by the time Emma walked in wearing one of the aprons. It had peace signs and flowers with big round petals all over it.

"Wow, that's fantastic!" Mia said.

"Spectacular!" I agreed. "Our booth is going to look very groovy."

Alexis joined us. "You know, we forgot to talk about how we're displaying them. I guess we can just use our round plastic trays." The trays are our go-to display method. They're supercheap to buy, and we can use them again and again. But thanks to Mom, I had something better.

"I almost forgot!" I said. I put down the cupcake I was icing and went into the front hallway, where I had dumped all my stuff. I came back into the kitchen carrying a box.

"You know how Mom likes to collect old things?" I asked. "Well, she has these vintage glass cake stands she said we could borrow. They're kind of sixties looking, right?"

"They're perfect!" Alexis said happily.

"I like how they're all different heights," Mia said. "That'll look cool when we set up the cupcakes."

Hearing that made me feel good, because now I felt like I had contributed something to the booth besides the cupcake design.

"We'll be done with the aprons in a little while," Emma said. "Then we'll come help you ice the cupcakes."

About an hour later, almost all the cupcakes were done and stored away in the plastic containers we use to keep them fresh and to transport them. Eddie and Dan came into the kitchen as we were finishing up.

"Got any for us to taste?" Eddie asked.

We actually learned early on that it's a good idea to taste our cupcakes before we serve them. Sometimes mistakes can happen that you can't see with your eyes—like not putting in enough sugar or adding too much salt, for example. So it's always good to have cupcake tasters on hand. For some reason, fathers and brothers seem to be very good at this.

Mia handed Eddie and Dan one cupcake each. Then we were all quiet as we watched them both take a bite.

Eddie grinned. "These are very good."

"Just very good?" Alexis asked. "Would you say they were award-winning cupcakes?"

"They're excellent!" Eddie said.

"Excellent isn't good enough," Mia said. "We need them to be spectacular."

"Well, they taste excellent and they look spectacular," Eddie said.

That seemed to satisfy everyone but Alexis, who turned to Dan.

"What do you think?" she asked him.

Dan shrugged. "What Dad said."

"Then I think we're good," I said. "Come on, let's finish up these last ones."

It was almost ten o'clock when we finally had everything cleaned up. Alexis's mom came to pick up Alexis and Emma. Alexis was furiously checking her to-do list as she was heading out the door.

"Cupcakes. Aprons. Milk. Straws. Tablecloth. Sign . . . sign!" she cried. "Oh no! We forgot to make a sign for the booth."

"Katie and I will do it," Mia promised.

Alexis sighed. "I'll see you guys in the morning."

She and Emma left, and I yawned. "We have to get up so early!"

"The sign won't take long," Mia reassured me. "I have all the stuff."

We changed into pj's and brushed our teeth, and then I dragged my sleeping bag up to Mia's room. Mia put a big piece of poster board on the floor and then brought out a shoe box filled with markers. I let Mia do all the drawing, because she's awesome at that, and then I helped color in all the bubble letters and flowers.

"Do you think we'll beat Callie and the BFC?" I asked, yawning.

"I don't know," Mia replied. "But we've done all we can. We'll have to wait and see."

I thought about what it would feel like to lose—and then have to go home with Callie after that.

"I really hope we win," I said.

I fell asleep in my sleeping bag on the floor, surrounded by a rainbow of markers.

CHAPTER 13

Some Very Suspicious School Spirit

$\mathcal{T}$he fund-raiser officially started at noon, but we decided we wanted to get to the school by ten thirty, so that we would have plenty of time to set up. Eddie made Mia and me a breakfast of omelets and toast. ("Because you worked so hard on those spectacular cupcakes," he told us.) Then Emma's mom drove up in their minivan at ten, with Emma and Alexis, and we loaded everything into the back.

There was no sign of Callie, Maggie, or Bella when we got to the fund-raiser. It was held in the school parking lot, and there were blue canopy tents, with tables underneath them, set up all over the lot. Each table was labeled with the name of a club, and we found the Cupcake Club table pretty quickly.

"We're near the front again," Alexis remarked. "That's good for business."

We got to work getting the booth ready right away. Mia's tie-dyed tablecloth looked fabulous on the table. I arranged Mom's cake platters, and Mia was right—the different heights looked cool. We put on our aprons and then worked together to carefully place the cupcakes on the stands. It's hard to do without getting icing on your fingers, and it's even harder to do without licking your fingers, which wouldn't be very hygienic.

Mr. Becker showed up around eleven thirty, wheeling a big cooler filled with milk bottles.

"Your table looks very nice, girls," he said.

"Thanks for getting the milk for us," I told him.

"I'm happy to support you guys," Alexis's dad replied. "You're all very ambitious. I have some other things for you too."

He unstrapped a cord that was wrapped around the cooler and gave Alexis a cardboard box.

"I had those flyers copied for you this morning," he said.

Alexis hugged him. "You're the best," she said. "When I'm CEO of my own company, you can be my assistant."

Mr. Becker laughed. "I don't think I would want

that job. I have a feeling it wouldn't be easy."

After he left, we all took a look at the flyers Alexis had made.

Having a Party or Special Event?
Serve Your Guests the Best Cupcakes in Town
Made Especially for You
by the Cupcake Club!
We have lots of different flavors and designs!

Underneath the words, there were pictures of some of the cupcakes we've made, and Alexis's cell phone number and the e-mail address we use for the club.

"This is great," I proclaimed. "We'll definitely get new business from this."

The last thing we needed to do was to put up our sign. We poked holes in the corners and then used string to hang it from the canopy poles behind the table. Then we stepped back to admire our work.

PEACE OUT!
Have a Groovy 50th Anniversary, Park Street!
Old School Cupcakes $2.00 • Milk $1.00
The Cupcake Club

The sign was decorated with flowers and peace signs, just like the aprons, and it looked really great. Then Emma's mom walked up with Jake.

"Wow, girls, this is wonderful!" she said. "Let me get a picture!"

Mia and I stood on one side of the table, and Alexis and Emma stood on the other, so we could make sure the cupcakes got in the picture. Of course, Jake ran over at the last minute, so he could be in it too. But he's short, so he didn't block the cupcakes.

"Okay, great," Mrs. Taylor said. "You girls had better get behind the table. You're going to be swamped soon."

She was right. People started swarming into the parking lot. Next to us, the Chess Club was charging people to challenge them at chess. On the other side of us, the school band had set up a funny photo booth. There wasn't any other food nearby, so the hungry people headed right for our cupcakes.

One of our first customers was Principal LaCosta. Even though it was Saturday, she was still dressed like a principal, in a navy blue suit and a pale yellow blouse. Her wavy brown hair was held in place by lots of hairspray, like it always is.

"Ah, the Cupcake Club!" she said. "I'm glad to

see you girls are still at it. And it's great to see that you're celebrating our school anniversary."

She bought one cupcake and one cup of milk. Alexis had a big smile on her face as she deposited the money into the cash box.

Other people liked the theme, too, especially parents.

"Tie-dyed cupcakes. Very groovy!" said one dad. Lots of people said stuff like that, or they flashed a peace sign at us.

We were really busy selling cupcakes for a while, and then I thought of something.

"Hey, we don't even know what kind of cupcakes the BFC has," I said, suddenly feeling worried again. They might be doing even better than we were.

Alexis frowned. "Maybe you and Mia should go check it out. Emma and I can handle this."

Mia and I made our way through the crowd. It wasn't hard to find the BFC booth, because it was the loudest booth in the place. They had a drummer, a trumpet player, and a flute player in front playing football fight songs.

As we got closer, we saw Maggie and Bella dressed as cheerleaders, waving blue-and-yellow pom-poms outside the booth.

"Get your school spirit here!" they were yelling.

Callie was dressed like a cheerleader too, and she was selling the cupcakes behind the BFC table. The cupcakes had white icing and maybe some cinnamon sprinkled on top.

"They didn't even do blue and yellow for school spirit," I remarked to Mia.

Beth Suzuki was walking by, and she heard me. "That's not the kind of school spirit they're talking about."

"What do you mean?" I asked.

"Some kids are saying the cupcakes taste like they have, you know, *spirits* in them," she said. "The kind that makes you drunk."

"That's ridiculous!" I sputtered. "Callie would never do that."

Beth shrugged. "Whatever. That's just what I heard." She walked away, and then we heard Maggie and Bella talking to Eddie Rossi, Wes Kinney, and some other boys about the cupcakes.

"Our cupcakes have lots of *spirit*," Maggie said, emphasizing the last word, and then she winked.

"I'll have ten!" Wes cried, and then he ran to the table.

Mia looked at me, and her eyes were wide. "I can't believe they're doing this!"

Then it hit me. "Wait, I recognize those cupcakes. Mrs. Wilson makes them for Christmas every year. She calls them rum ball cupcakes, but she uses imitation rum extract. I know because my mom told me. I've been eating them since I was little. They taste like rum, but there's no alcohol in them."

"Maybe. But they're trying to make everyone *think* there is," Mia pointed out.

"We'd better tell Alexis and Emma," I said, and we made our way back to the booth.

Emma and Alexis were shocked after we reported what the BFC were doing.

"So *that's* their secret plan," Alexis said. "They must think they'll sell tons of cupcakes if everyone thinks there's alcohol in them."

"Well, it's working," Emma said, glancing at their booth. "Look!"

There was a long line at the BFC stand, mostly made up of boys.

Alexis shook her head. "This is so unfair."

"I guess, but they're not really doing anything wrong, are they?" I asked. "We knew they were going to do something big. So we've just got to try harder, that's all."

"Katie's right," Mia said. She cupped her hands around her mouth. "Get your groovy cupcakes

here! Tie-dyed cupcakes! You've never seen anything like them!"

I joined in. "See how delicious peace can be!"
I yelled. "Give peace a chance!" I knew I sounded
silly, but I had to say something. I wasn't going to
let the BFC win!

CHAPTER 14

Big Trouble for the BFC

For the next hour I stayed focused on selling. I poured milk. Mia and Emma handed out cupcakes, and Alexis worked the cash box. I tried not to think of all the great business the BFC was getting, but it was hard not to. Those marching band kids kept playing the same school spirit songs over and over.

"That music is making me crazy!" I cried. "I wish we had our own band. Then we could drown them out."

"Hey, I have an idea," Mia said. She took out her cell phone and then nodded to Emma. "Be right back."

A few minutes later Mia came back with a big smile on her face, but she didn't say what she was planning. After about fifteen minutes her stepdad showed up with one of those boom-box docking stations. He popped in an iPod.

"Where do you want this, Mia?" Eddie asked.

"On the end of the table," she said. "And crank it up!"

Eddie nodded and then turned on the iPod, and a song by the Beatles started playing.

Mia grinned. "Eddie has a whole playlist of sixties songs. Perfect, right?"

"Glad I could help," Eddie said. "How are your sales going?"

I glanced at the table. A lot of cake stands were empty.

"We've sold one hundred and thirty-two cupcakes, but we've got to sell them *all* if we're going to meet our total from last year," Alexis reported.

"Don't forget the milk," Emma reminded her.

"Oh, that's right!" Alexis said. She looked down at her notepad. "We've sold fifty-nine cups of milk."

I looked in the cooler. "We're almost out of milk," I reported. "And we still need to recycle the bottles before the end of the fund-raiser."

Eddie gave us a funny little bow. "At your service, ladies. I'm going to walk around. Give a yell when you want me to take them back to the store for you."

As Mia's stepdad started to walk away, he stopped and did a goofy dance to the music. Mia groaned and rolled her eyes. "Stop! Please! You're going to drive away all our customers!"

Eddie smiled and danced away. He might have been goofy, but the music got the attention of more of the parents. Pretty soon the booth was nice and crowded again.

George even came to the booth with his friend Ken. George started doing this wacky dance to the music, waving his arms in the air and everything. I was cracking up.

Then he walked up to me. "All that dancing made me thirsty. Can I have some milk, please?" He held out a crumpled dollar bill.

"Sure. You need to pay Alexis," I told him as I handed him a cup of milk and a straw.

George took a long, loud slurp of milk. "Mmm, milky!" he said. Then he was quiet for a little bit, like he was going to say something. Finally he said, "So, Katie, you're going to the dance, right?"

I nodded. "Yup."

"Cool," he said. "I guess I'll see you there, then."

And then he paid Alexis, and he and Ken walked away.

Mia looked at me and wiggled her eyebrows.

"Do *not* say it!" I warned her.

Then Emma tapped me on the shoulder. "Hey, look over there!"

Principal LaCosta and Mr. Hammond, the school's vice principal, were marching toward the BFC booth, and they looked angry. The marching band kids stopped playing, but we still couldn't hear what anyone was saying. Principal LaCosta was talking to all the customers, and then all the customers started walking away! Then Maggie and Bella and Callie were talking to Principal LaCosta. Everyone looked very upset. Callie even looked like she might start to cry. I saw Principal LaCosta shaking her head and frowning. She said a few more words to the girls and pointed to the booth. To our amazement, Callie and the BFC started packing up their cupcakes!

The marching band's flute player walked by our booth, so I quickly approached her.

"Hey, what happened to the BFC booth?" I asked.

"Principal LaCosta said the theme of the booth was inappropriate," the girl told me with a shrug. "I thought it was just school spirit. But I guess some kids think there's alcohol in the cupcakes."

I turned back to my friends. "Whoa. Can you believe it?"

"Of course I can," Alexis said. "It doesn't matter if there's alcohol in the cupcakes or not. You can't promote alcohol at a middle school fund-raiser. I'm sure they're in big trouble."

I looked over to the booth and saw Principal LaCosta and Mr. Hammond leading the girls into the school, probably to the principal's office. I felt a twinge of sympathy for Callie . . . but that quickly went away when the BFC's cupcake customers came to our booth instead. It was amazing. We were slammed, and we were sold out of cupcakes in about fifteen minutes.

"This is fantastic!" Alexis said, counting the money. "We made four hundred and sixty-seven dollars—that's more than last year! And that's not even counting the money from the recycled bottles."

"I'll get Eddie!" Mia said, and she sped off to look for him.

I was feeling pretty excited. It looked like we were going to win—again! And then Mrs. Wilson walked up to the booth.

"There you are, Katie," she said. "Listen, I'm afraid we need to leave a little early. I got a call from Principal LaCosta about Callie."

"I know," I said, awkwardly averting her eyes. I felt kind of embarrassed for Callie.

"I have to go get her, and we'll come pick you up on the way to the car, okay?" she asked.

I nodded. "Sorry, guys," I said, turning to Emma and Alexis. "I'll clean up as much as I can before she gets back."

It turns out I had plenty of time to clean up. Principal LaCosta must have had a lot to say to everybody. Mrs. Wilson came back to the booth with Callie about four feet behind her, ignoring us. Her eyes were red, and I could tell she had been crying.

"Ready, Katie?" Mrs. Wilson asked.

"Sure," I said. I went behind the table and grabbed my overnight bag and backpack. Then I followed Mrs. Wilson and Callie out of the parking lot. I packed my stuff into the trunk and slid into the backseat. Callie was in the front seat with her mom, which was a relief. I sat back and tried to act invisible.

"Mom, this is so unfair," Callie wailed. "You know there's no alcohol in those cupcakes."

"I do know that, Callie, but as Principal LaCosta said, that's not the real problem," Mrs. Wilson told her. "The problem is that you tried to make kids *think* there was alcohol in them."

"It's not my fault if people thought that," Callie replied. "I can't control what other people think."

"Principal LaCosta says you and Maggie and Bella were the ones spreading the rumor," said Mrs. Wilson.

"And you believe *her* and not your own daughter?" Callie cried indignantly.

I knew Principal LaCosta was right, because I had seen it myself. But I didn't say anything. Callie was in big enough trouble as it was.

Mrs. Wilson sighed. "That's enough, Callie. We'll talk more about this with your father."

Callie started to cry again, and now I felt *really* awkward. I felt like I should say something to comfort her, but I figured anything I said might just make her mad. So I kept quiet.

Boy, this is going to be a really fun weekend! I thought.

CHAPTER 15

Believe It or Not, Things Get Worse!

A few minutes later we pulled up in front of Callie's house. Callie quickly got out of the front seat and slammed the door behind her—hard. Then she walked through the front gate and slammed that behind her. Then she walked through the front door and—you guessed it—slammed that behind her too.

Mrs. Wilson did not look happy as she opened the trunk for me.

"Um, where should I put my bags?" I asked as she walked in the house.

"In Callie's room," she replied. "We pulled out the daybed for you this morning."

I'm sure I turned as pale as vanilla icing when I heard that. Callie's room! Mrs. Wilson actually expected us to stay in the same room! *Ugh!*

Maybe Mrs. Wilson didn't realize how bad things were between me and Callie. Or maybe, like my mom, she was choosing to ignore it. I think they still thought of us as little girls who had sleepovers together. I didn't even bother to argue with her.

I sighed and then walked to the staircase as Mr. Wilson came out of the kitchen wearing a big apron. (Only a big apron would fit him, because he kind of reminds me of a grizzly bear.)

"Katie! Where have you been? You look like you've grown a foot over the summer!" Mr. Wilson said. Then he gave me a big hug.

Remember I told you how Callie and I have known each other since we were babies? Well, that means I've known her parents for that long too. Mr. Wilson was always kind of like a father to me, which was nice, because I never see my natural father. But since Callie dumped me, I never get to see my second father either. That's another reason why what Callie did hurts so much.

I started to answer him, but Callie's mom interrupted us. "Joe, we need to talk," she said in a serious voice.

Mr. Wilson nodded. "See you later, Katie. I'm

making my famous spaghetti for dinner. Hope you're hungry!"

Normally I love Mr. Wilson's spaghetti, but the thought of having to stay in Callie's room made me lose my appetite. I slowly dragged my bags up the stairs and knocked on Callie's door. She didn't answer at first, so I knocked again.

"What do you want?" she finally asked.

"Your mom says I'm sleeping in here," I said.

After a minute, Callie opened the door and then walked back over to her bed without saying a word to me. She was furiously texting someone on her cell phone—Maggie and Bella, I'm sure.

"So, I guess I'll just put down my stuff," I said, and Callie ignored me again.

I placed my bags on the daybed, which had been pulled out from under Callie's bed and was closer to the floor. I didn't know what to do, so I pulled out my cell phone to text my mom.

How's grandma? I texted. Is she out of surgery yet?

Not yet, my mom texted back. I'll let you know the minute I hear anything.

I put down my phone and looked around Callie's room. She still had lots of posters on her walls, mostly of cute boys from magazines. Then I noticed the picture of me and Callie from when we were kids was missing from the top of her dresser.

That made me mad and sad at the same time. I needed to hear from one of my *true* friends.

Help me! I texted Mia.

I turned my back to Callie's bed, to make sure she couldn't see.

I'm trapped in Callie's room! I have to sleep here!

Everyone is talking about the BFC, Mia texted back. They really messed up.

I know, I replied. Can you believe it? Callie is worse than Sydney!

Then Mr. Wilson called down to us. "Girls! Time for spaghetti!"

I quickly shut my cell phone. Callie climbed down from her bed and almost stepped on me as she headed out. I slowly followed her.

Downstairs, the kitchen table was set for four. There was a big bowl of salad, a bigger bowl of spaghetti, and a basket of bread.

"Let's dig in!" Mr. Wilson said.

"Where's Jenna?" I asked. Callie's older sister is a senior in high school.

"She's working at the mall," Mrs. Wilson told me. "She got a job in that clothing store that sells all the jeans."

"Cool," I said, and I sat down.

Mr. Wilson took my plate and piled it high with food. It smelled delicious, but I still wasn't that hungry. To be polite, I started picking at it with my fork. Callie wasn't even trying. She just sat there with her arms crossed. Mr. Wilson sighed. "Callie, I think we need to talk about what happened today," he said.

"Not in front of Katie," Callie said, glaring at me.

"I can, um, eat somewhere else," I said.

Callie's dad sighed again. "No, let's eat. Callie, we can talk after dinner."

Now Callie glared at him. She didn't eat a bite, but I have to admit that the delicious smell got to me. I ate at least half of the giant mound of spaghetti on my plate.

"Thanks, Mr. Wilson," I said when I was done. "That was really good."

"Katie, why don't you go upstairs and get ready for the dance?" Mrs. Wilson suggested.

"Sure," I said.

I headed upstairs, and the first thing I did was brush my teeth, because I am the daughter of a dentist. (Besides, who wants spaghetti breath?) Then I went into Callie's room and opened up my overnight bag.

Last year, Mia went to the mall with me to help me pick out the perfect dress, which became my favorite purple dress. But my purple dress was too short, and I totally forgot to go out and get a new one.

In case you didn't already know, I don't really know much about fashion. I put stuff on, and if I like it, I leave it on. When I packed, I kind of just grabbed a bunch of stuff. One of the things I grabbed was my second-favorite dress—this dress I wear in the summer. It has straps instead of sleeves and a kind of orange-and-pink tie-dyed pattern. Since it was still hot out, I thought it might be okay to wear. But now I worried that maybe it was too summery.

I sighed and put it on. It was the only dress I packed. But I had no idea what else to wear with it.

I wish Mia were here! I thought.

Then I had an idea. I took a picture of myself and texted her.

Help again! I said. What should I wear with this?

Mia didn't hesitate. Do u have ur white flats?

I quickly checked my bag. Yes! I had them.

Yes! I said.

Good. Wear those. Any sweaters? Mia asked.

I looked through my bag again.

Green with short sleeves or white with long sleeves, I wrote.

Try the green, Mia texted back.

I wasn't sure if the green would go with orange and pink, but then again, I love to wear lots of colors together. I tried it on, took another picture, and texted Mia. I had to admit that it looked pretty good.

Great! she replied. Will bring a necklace 4 u that'll look great with your outfit.

Then my phone started to ring. It was my mom.

Gotta go, I texted, then I answered the phone.

"Hi, sweetie, how's it going?" Mom asked.

"How's Grandma?" I asked her back.

I heard Callie's footsteps on the stairs, so I quickly left her bedroom. I went into the bathroom and then closed the door behind me.

"She's doing great!" Mom said, and she sounded happy and relieved. "She's awake and alert. The doctors say the surgery went well, and she can go home in a few days."

"That's great!" I said. I suddenly felt a lot lighter, as though a huge weight had been lifted from my shoulders. I didn't realize how much I had been secretly worrying about Grandma until Mom said she was going to be all right.

"So how did the fund-raiser go?" Mom asked.

"Well . . . ," I began, and then I told her the whole story.

"That's terrible!" Mom said. "You and I know that Callie would never put alcohol in cupcakes."

"I know, Mom," I said. "But I guess they're in trouble because . . . well . . . it's complicated."

"Did you tell Principal LaCosta that you make those cupcakes with her every year?" Mom asked.

"No," I said.

"You could vouch for her, Katie," Mom said. "That's what friends do."

"But we're not friends anymore, Mom," I said, and my voice was angry. "I keep telling you that!"

Mom was quiet for a minute. "Well, you used to be," she finally said. "I'm surprised at you, Katie. Keeping quiet is the same thing as not sticking up for someone. You would want her to do the same thing for you."

"But *she* wouldn't!" I said, and I know my voice was really loud—that's how upset I was. "She's changed, Mom! She's mean and terrible, and she wouldn't stick up for me. Ever!" Why couldn't she just understand?

Mom sighed. "Just because Callie isn't behaving nicely, doesn't mean that you shouldn't."

"I guess," I said, but I did not feel like being nice to Callie right now. She got herself into this mess— and now she'd have to deal with it.

CHAPTER 16

Everybody's Talking

When I opened the bathroom door, Callie was standing there. I felt scared for a second. Had she heard what I said to my mom?

"Are you done yet?" Callie asked in a really snotty voice.

"Yeah," I replied, and I quickly went down the stairs.

Mr. and Mrs. Wilson were waiting in the living room.

"Katie, you look so pretty!" Callie's mom exclaimed.

"Thanks," I said.

Mr. Wilson shook his head. "I can't believe how fast you girls are growing up. When Callie comes down, I'll take a picture of you both."

So we waited for Callie to get dressed. And we waited. Finally, Mrs. Wilson yelled up the stairs.

"Callie, are you ready yet?" she called out.

Callie stomped down the stairs wearing sweat-pants and a T-shirt.

"I'm not going," she said, flopping down on the sofa. "It was unfair, and we aren't going to win, so what's the point?"

Mr. Wilson shook his head. "You're not being a good sport, Callie."

"Honestly, Callie, I had to plead with Principal LaCosta not to ban you from the dance," Mrs. Wilson said. She sounded really frustrated. "And now you're not going to go?"

Callie shrugged. "You can't make me."

Mrs. Wilson looked at her husband, and they must be telepathic or something, because the next thing I knew, Mr. Wilson said, "Okay, Katie. Looks like it's just you and me. I'll give you a ride."

Riding to the dance without Callie was pretty awkward, but I was also relieved to be away from her for a while.

"I'm sorry about Callie's behavior tonight," Mr. Wilson said. "She just hasn't been herself this year."

"Yeah, I know," I agreed. And then the next

thing just slipped out. "Or last year, either."

Mr. Wilson nodded. "Callie's having a hard time figuring out where she belongs," he said. "She's still the same Callie, though."

I didn't agree with him, but I didn't say anything. I was really glad when he pulled up in front of the school.

"Your mom arranged for Emma's mom to drop you off after the dance," he said. "See you later, and have a good time!"

"Thanks," I said, and then I headed inside the school gym.

The place was packed with middle school kids and the parents who were chaperoning. This year, there was a big blue-and-yellow balloon archway over the dj table that looked really cool. Blue-and-yellow crepe paper was strung all across the ceiling.

I spotted Emma, Alexis, and Mia over by the watercoolers. Emma had a pink headband in her hair, and she wore this really cute white dress with tiny pink flowers on it. Mia looked superfashionable, as always, in a dress with a big red-and-purple pattern. (She told me later it's called color blocking.) And Alexis's curly hair was straightened, and she had on a black dress, and her heels were kind of high.

"Let me guess," I said. "Dylan got to you."

Alexis nodded. "I couldn't escape."

"Well, I think you look nice," I said. "You look like you're in high school."

Alexis blushed. "Thanks!"

"You all look nice," I said.

"You do too," Emma told me.

I looked at Mia. "Thanks to you. If I didn't have my own personal fashion consultant, I'd be lost."

Mia laughed. "Hey, you're my first client! And here's the necklace I promised you." She put it on me, and she was right—it was perfect.

As we were talking, I got that weird feeling someone was looking at me. (Has that ever happened to you?) When I turned around, I saw that Maggie and Bella were sitting at a table, and they were surrounded by a bunch of girls. The girls were pointing and whispering.

I frowned. "What's that about?" I asked my friends.

"They've been talking to anyone who'll listen," Alexis said. "They keep saying the whole contest was fixed."

"That's crazy," I said. "They ruined things for themselves."

Then I heard Maggie get really loud. "Principal

LaCosta just didn't want us to win," she said. "We were beating the Cupcake Club, and she didn't want to see her teacher's pets lose."

"I wouldn't be surprised if those Cupcake girls were the ones who told on you," said one of the girls at the table.

I was getting really mad. "That is ridiculous!" I said.

"They can talk all they want," Alexis said. "We raised almost five hundred dollars. We're definitely winning."

But the idea of winning didn't seem so important anymore—especially if people didn't think we deserved it. I spotted Principal LaCosta over by the food table, and I decided to do something, right then and there.

"Be right back," I told my friends.

Usually I would be afraid to talk to Principal LaCosta, but I guess I was just feeling tired of all the rumors and lies and stuff.

"Principal LaCosta, can I talk to you, please?" I asked.

She turned and saw me. "Oh, hi, Katie. Of course."

"It's about the Best Friends Club's cupcakes," I said. "I used to make those cupcakes with Callie every year, and I know there's no rum in them. She uses imitation rum extract. So maybe you could let them back in the contest. I know they sold a lot of cupcakes, and if they sold the most, then they deserve to win."

"It's nice of you to stand up for your friend," Principal LaCosta said. "But the girls' parents already told me about the imitation rum. That's not the issue here. The issue is we simply can't have students promoting alcohol use, even if they're just joking about it. Do you understand?"

I nodded. Mrs. Wilson had said the same thing.

"Thanks," I said, and then I felt nervous for real, so I walked away. I noticed Maggie and Bella staring at me, and I wondered if they had heard.

I hoped they did, but it didn't matter. I stood up for Callie, and I felt a lot better.

Then Mia ran up and grabbed my arm. "I love this song!" she cried, and then we were all dancing, and suddenly things were fun again.

CHAPTER 17

One Mystery Is Solved

There's a funny thing that happens at a middle school dance. When it starts, most of the girls stay on the left side of the gym, and most of the boys hang out on the right side of the gym. The girls dance with girls, and the boys dance with boys. Then, as the night goes on, everyone starts dancing with one another, boys and girls together. And sometimes boys even ask girls to dance.

About halfway through the dance, I was standing around talking to my friends. Sophie and Lucy were with us, and Beth came over with some girls who I think are all into art, because they were dressed really funky, like Beth. Anyway, we were just talking and laughing and having a good time when the subject turned to boys.

"We need more cute boys in this school!" Sophie was wailing.

"I think Eddie Rossi is cute," admitted Lucy, and Sophie looked shocked.

"He's, like, two feet taller than you!" Sophie squealed.

"Eddie has a crush on Katie," Alexis blurted out, and I felt my face get red.

"Alexis! He does not!" I protested.

"Well, I think George Martinez has a crush on Katie," Sophie said.

I wished I could turn invisible. "How do you know that?" I asked her.

"Because he's waving at you," Sophie said, pointing across the gym.

I looked, and Sophie was right. George was walking toward us, and he was smiling and waving at us.

Mia grabbed my arm. "Oh my gosh! He's going to ask you to dance!"

"He is not!" I said, but secretly I hoped she was right. Or wrong. I'm not sure! I was so nervous.

Before George could get there, Eddie Rossi walked up from the other direction. And he was walking right toward me.

My friends were stunned. Mia was practically pulling off my arm. I could tell she was dying to say something, but thankfully everyone kept quiet.

"Hey, Katie," Eddie said. "I . . . I've been meaning to talk to you about something since school started."

My heart was pounding so fast. "Oh?"

Eddie nodded. "Yeah, it's kind of hard to explain, but . . . well, I want to apologize to you."

That was definitely not what I thought he was going to say!

"Apologize for what?" I asked, confused.

"For the way I made fun of you last year in gym class," Eddie said. He took a deep breath. "I went to camp this summer with my little brother, and he got teased a lot. It was hard to see. And then we had this whole meeting where we learned about bullying and stuff, and I realized that I did it too."

I was shocked by Eddie's confession. I didn't think people could change like that.

"I'm sorry your brother got bullied," I said.

"Thanks. And I'm sorry too," Eddie said. "For the stuff I said to you. That's one of the things they told us. That it's never too late to apologize."

"Everything's cool," I told him. "I really appreciate how you've been sticking up for me lately."

"I'll have your back from now on," Eddie promised.

I smiled. "Thanks. I could use it!" I was totally relieved that he didn't like me in the way everybody thought. He was just trying to make up for his past behavior.

From the corner of my eye, I saw George turn around and walk away. I was going to call out to him, but then Eddie said, "See ya, Katie," and he was gone too.

I turned to Mia. "What just happened?"

"Maybe George thought Eddie was asking you to dance," she said.

"But he wasn't," I said. "Eddie doesn't even like me. He's just nicer now, that's all."

That's when I realized that I was disappointed. And *that* meant I *wanted* to dance with George. Wow. Scary.

Then the microphone next to the dj table was turned on, and Principal LaCosta started to talk. The gym got quiet.

"Hello, Park Street Middle School!" she cried, and everyone clapped. "Today's fund-raiser was a big success. We raised almost three thousand dollars!"

Everyone cheered really loud at that.

"And the club that raised the most money . . . for the second year in a row . . . is the Cupcake Club!" she announced.

We all started squealing and hugging one another. I couldn't believe it. We had done it again!

We ran up to the dj booth, and Principal LaCosta handed each of us a blue-and-yellow Park Street Middle School blanket. Last year we got sweatshirts. I guess she's trying to keep us warm.

I wore my blanket like a cape and started spinning and twirling on the dance floor.

"Hey, Supergirl!"

It was George. He started spinning around like I was. We kept dancing like that and laughing. I'm sure we looked totally goofy.

Bella and Maggie walked by.

"It's so unfair," Maggie said, loudly enough for me to hear. "Definitely not a fair fight!"

I could have said something back, but I didn't. Instead, I just kept on spinning with George.

CHAPTER 18

A Sweet Ending

By the time the dance was over I was super-exhausted and happy. I wrapped my winning blanket around me as I rode back to Callie's in the back of Emma's car. Alexis and Mia were squished in with me.

"I wish you could go home with me," Mia said.

"Me too," I said. "But it's just a few more nights."

"Text me any time, okay?" Mia said.

"Me too," added Alexis.

"And me," said Emma.

"You guys are the best!" I said with a yawn.

"Okay, Katie, this is your stop," Mrs. Taylor announced.

"Thanks, Mrs. Taylor!" I said, and I climbed out of the car.

The porch light was on, and Mrs. Wilson was waiting for me with the door open.

"How was the dance, Katie?" she asked.

"It was good," I said.

"Callie's up in her bedroom," she told me. "I'm not sure if she's awake or not, so you might want to be quiet."

"Okay," I said. It would perfect if Callie was asleep. Then I wouldn't have to talk to her.

But I was not so lucky. Callie was in bed with the lights off, but she was sitting up with her cell phone on.

"Oh, hey," Callie said.

"Hey," I said back. I started digging in my bag for my pajamas.

Callie turned on the little lamp on her nightstand. She looked like she had calmed down a lot from how she'd been before the dance. Because I've known Callie forever, I know she doesn't usually stay mad for very long. At least the *old* Callie didn't stay mad for very long. A few moments went by, and then she started asking questions. I knew she was dying to find out what happened at the dance.

"So, what dress did Mia wear?" she asked.

"It was color blocked," I said, glad that Mia had told me so I had something to say. "Purple and red."

Callie nodded. "Cool. Did Jeremy Paskowski dance with anybody?"

I shrugged. "I don't know him."

"He's that tall blond-haired kid on the basketball team," Callie said.

I could sort of picture him. "Um, I don't think so."

Then Callie blurted out, "I know why you didn't stick up for me."

"I *did* stick up for you," I told her. "I explained to Principal LaCosta tonight that those aren't really rum cupcakes. I asked her to include the sales you made in the contest. But she said no."

Callie looked surprised. "Why did you do that?"

"I'm not sure," I confessed. "But it was the right thing to do. We used to be good friends."

We were quiet again, until Callie spoke up.

"You won, right?" she asked.

I nodded. "Yes."

"Peace Out was a good theme," Callie said.

"So was school spirit," I told her. "It was cool that you had a band and everything."

More silence.

"I'm really sorry about how things turned out," Callie said finally.

I wasn't expecting that. Callie was apologizing?

I wasn't sure what to say. It turns out that was okay, because Callie kept talking. "I'm sorry I didn't stick up for you to Sydney, and I'm sorry I didn't treat you like a friend."

"Okay," I said, because I still didn't know what else to say.

"Sydney had all these rules about who we should talk to and who we shouldn't, but I think that's stupid," Callie went on. "I can talk to or be friends with whoever I like. And I don't have to be mean to other people in order to be popular."

That was interesting. But I guess it made sense. That's probably why she changed the club name after all.

"But you're going to stay in the club?" I asked.

"Well, sure!" replied Callie. "I like it."

I didn't know what to say. But letting Callie do all the talking was working out pretty well for me so far, so I just nodded.

"Things are just different," Callie said after a while. "I changed the name of the club because I realized Sydney was pretty horrible. I liked the idea of the club, but not what the club was. It will be different this year."

I sighed. I really wanted to believe Callie, but with all that hair flipping and stuff, she didn't seem that much different from Sydney to me. And I didn't really like Maggie or Bella all that much. And their whole club was pretty silly.

But Callie had apologized. That was pretty big.

"Truce?" Callie asked.

"Truce," I agreed.

Callie held out her hand. "Shake on it," she said. "So we can Peace Out."

I laughed, and we shook hands. Then I grabbed my pajamas.

"I'm going to get changed," I told her.

As I brushed my teeth, I thought about everything that had happened. What a crazy day! The Cupcake Club won the contest. I figured out the mystery of Eddie Rossi. I danced with George, kind of. Grandma Carole was okay. And the war with Callie looked like it was over. . . . And that all happened without my lucky purple dress or lucky purple shirt or even my lucky nail polish. I felt relieved. I felt, well, peaceful. I guess that theme worked out well in more ways than one.

I smiled at my reflection in the mirror.

Maybe this was going to be my best, grooviest middle school year after all!

Want another sweet cupcake?

Here's a sneak peek
of the tenth book in the

CUPCAKE DIARIES

series:

Mia's

boiling point

A Middle School Miracle?

Oh my gosh, it's a cupcake plunger!" my friend Katie squealed.

I don't think I've ever seen Katie so excited. We were in a shop in the mall called Baker's Hollow. They sell baking supplies, and inside are all these fake trees with shelves built into them and the supplies are displayed on them.

Katie and I were at one of the cupcake trees that has fake pretty pink cupcakes growing in its fake branches. The shelves were filled with cupcake baking pans, cupcake decorations, and tons of different kinds of cupcake liners.

Katie was holding up a metal tube with a purple top on it. She pulled on the top and it moved up and down, like a plunger.

"This is so cool!" she cried. "You stick this in the top of the cupcake and plunge halfway down, and a perfect little tube of cake comes out. Then you fill the hole with stuff and then put the cake back on top and frost it. Just imagine what you could put in here! Whipped cream! Pudding!"

She turned to me, and her brown eyes were shining with excitement. "You could even do ice cream! Can you imagine biting into a cupcake and there's ice cream inside? How awesome would that be?"

"Totally awesome," I agreed. "Plus, it's purple. Your favorite color."

Katie dug into her pocket, took out some crumpled bills, and started to count.

"It's only six dollars. I could get it and still have enough left over for a smoothie," she said, and then she sighed. "I am so glad they opened this store, but I am going to go broke spending all my money on cupcake supplies. I'm obsessed!"

"I know how you feel," I said. "I am totally obsessed with shoes lately. I'm trying to find the perfect pair of neutral heels. I want them dressy, but not too dressy—maybe a shiny patent leather, with a high heel. But not too high, I don't want to fall flat on my face! I can picture them in my mind, but I haven't seen them anywhere "for real" yet."

Katie looked down at her sneakers, which were decorated with rainbows drawn on with colored markers. "I don't think I'll ever wear heels. They're too uncomfortable."

That's the difference between me and Katie—she doesn't care about fashion at all, and I pretty much live for it. Like today, Katie was wearing a purple hoodie, jeans, and sneakers. Which is perfectly adorable on her, but not dressed up enough for me. You never know who you could run into at the mall! So I had on black skinny jeans, my furry black boots, a white lace cami, and a sky blue cardigan on top. The beads in my hoop earrings matched my cardigan, and the boho style of the earrings worked perfectly with my boots.

But even though Katie doesn't care much about fashion, she's my best friend here in Maple Grove. I moved here after my parents got divorced. Katie was the first friend I met.

"Okay, I'd better get on line before I buy something else," she told me.

A few minutes later we left the shop and Katie was happily holding an adorable little paper shopping bag with a picture of a cupcake tree on it.

"That's such a great logo," I said. "I wish I had thought of that for the Cupcake Club."

"I bet you could think of an even better logo if you wanted to," Katie said.

That made me feel pretty good. I love to draw and would love to be a fashion designer or maybe a graphic designer one day. Or maybe one of those designers who does displays in store windows in Manhattan. How cool would that be?

As we walked toward the smoothie shop, the smell of chocolate distracted us. Katie and I didn't even need to discuss it. We walked right into Adele's Chocolates and headed for the counter.

This is a "must-go-to" shop at the mall. Adele makes all of the chocolates herself, and the flavors are amazing.

"Mmm, look," I said, pointing to a glistening morsel of chocolate in a gold wrapper. "Salted caramel. That sounds so good."

Katie pointed to a piece of dark chocolate nestled in a pale purple wrapper. "Dark chocolate infused with lavender. I wonder what that tastes like."

"That would make a good cupcake," I said, and Katie nodded. We talk about cupcakes a lot because we're in the Cupcake Club with our friends Alexis and Emma. It's a real business. People hire us to bake for their parties and other events.

Katie had a pained look on her face. "Soooo tempting. But I think I really need some smoothie energy right about now. Mom says chocolate makes me loopy."

I grabbed Katie's arm and pretended to drag her out of the store. "Resist! Resist!" I said, and we both started laughing like crazy.

"We should go right to the smoothie place," I said, when we calmed down. "No more distractions."

"Right," Katie said. She stood up straight like a soldier, and saluted. "To the smoothie place!"

It was Saturday, so the mall was pretty crowded as we made our way to Smoothie Paradise. I used to hate the mall when I first moved here, because I was so used to shopping in New York City. But now I like it. It's never too hot or too cold, and when I'm done shopping I just have to carry the bags outside to Mom's car. It's definitely a lot easier than toting things home on the subway.

Even though the mall was crowded, the line at Smoothie Paradise was pretty short. Katie and I each ordered the same thing—a smoothie with mango and passion fruit—and then sat down at a small round table in the corner.

"This is my favorite kind of day," Katie said, after taking a long slurp from her straw. "I got all of my homework done last night, so I don't have anything to worry about."

Mia nodded. "Me too."

Katie sat back in her chair. "You know, the second year of middle school isn't so bad so far. I mean, it's not perfect, but I think it's easier than last year was."

"Definitely," I agreed. "It's like, we know our way around. And besides school, other things are easier too. Like living with Eddie and Dan. That's not so weird anymore."

Eddie is my stepdad, and Dan is my stepbrother. They're both pretty nice.

"Is it getting any easier living in two different homes?" Katie asked.

I thought about it for a minute. "Yeah, kind of," I admitted. "But mostly when I go to my dad's I feel like I'm visiting." I basically go out to see my dad every other weekend.

"You must miss him," Katie said.

I wasn't sure how to answer that. Katie's parents are divorced too, and she never sees her dad. He remarried, and I think he even has a whole new family. So as tough as my situation is, I think Katie's is even tougher.

I decided to be honest. "Sometimes I miss him," I said. "But he texts me and Skypes me and stuff during the week. So he's there if I need him."

Katie got a little quiet after I said that, so I changed the subject.

"We should go to Icon after this," I said. Katie knows that's my favorite clothing store. "They sell shoes there, too. Maybe they have my perfect heels."

We left the shop and headed for Icon. It's easy to find because you can hear techno music blasting from it even when the mall is noisy. The decor is really sleek and clean, with white walls and gleaming silver racks. I like it that way because the clothes are really highlighted.

That day I walked right past the clothes and headed straight for the shoes, which were displayed on white blocks sticking out of the back wall. They had chunky heels, wedge heels, and spike heels, but the perfect shoe, the one I could picture in my head, wasn't there.

While I was looking at all the shoes, Katie was giggling and wobbling in a pair of superhigh silver heels. I suddenly heard a familiar voice behind us.

"Hi, Mia. Hi, Katie."

It was Callie Wilson, Katie's former best friend and the leader of the Best Friends Club, which used to be the Popular Girls Club. Things have always been pretty tense between the Cupcake Club and the BFC. A lot of it had to do with Katie and Callie's broken friendship. But recently, they kind of patched things up, and so today Callie was smiling and friendly.

Katie, on the other hand, looked a little startled. She quickly slipped out of the silver heels, embarrassed.

"Oh hey, Callie," Katie said.

"Hi," I added.

Maggie and Bella, the other two girls in the BFC, walked up behind Callie. Maggie has wild hair and can be pretty funny when she wants to be—and pretty mean, too. Bella is the quietest of the three. She's super into those vampire movies—

like, so into them that she changed her name from Brenda to Bella, and she straightens her auburn hair to look just like the girl who loves the vampire.

"Shopping for shoes?" Callie asked, even though it was pretty obvious. I guess she was trying to make conversation.

"I'm trying to find the perfect pair of heels," I said. "But I think they only exist in my head."

"Ooh, I saw this adorable pair online," Maggie said. She whipped out her smartphone and started typing on the keyboard. Then she shoved the screen in front of my face. "See?"

"Those are totally cute, but the ones I'm dreaming of have a pointier toe," I told her. "But thanks!"

"Did you guys see those new wrap dresses they got in?" Callie asked. "Katie, there's a purple one that would look so cute on you."

"We'll definitely check them out," I replied.

"Yeah," Katie added.

Callie gave a little wave and then flipped her long, blond hair over her shoulder. "Okay, we've got to go. Later."

She walked away, and Bella and Maggie followed her. Katie and I stared at each other in shock.

"Did that just actually happen?" Katie asked.

"You mean did we actually just have a normal conversation with the BFC, with no name calling or teasing? Yes!" I replied.

Katie grinned. "It's a miracle!"

Coco Simon always dreamed of opening a cupcake bakery but was afraid she would eat all of the profits. When she's not daydreaming about cupcakes, Coco edits children's books and has written close to one hundred books for children, tweens, and young adults, which is a lot less than the number of cupcakes she's eaten. Cupcake Diaries is the first time Coco has mixed her love of cupcakes with writing.

Still Hungry?
There's always room for another Cupcake!

Katie and the Cupcake Cure
978-1-4424-2275-9 $5.99
978-1-4424-2276-6 (eBook)

Mia in the Mix
978-1-4424-2277-3 $5.99
978-1-4424-2278-0 (eBook)

Emma on Thin Icing
978-1-4424-2279-7 $5.99
978-1-4424-2280-3 (eBook)

Alexis and the Perfect Recipe
978-1-4424-2901-7 $5.99
978-1-4424-2902-4 (eBook)

Katie, Batter Up!
978-1-4424-4611-3 $5.99
978-1-4424-4612-0 (eBook)

Mia's Baker's Dozen

978-1-4424-4613-7 $5.99
978-1-4424-4614-4 (eBook)

Emma All Stirred Up!

978-1-4424-5078-3 $5.99
978-1-4424-5079-0 (eBook)

Alexis Cool as a Cupcake

978-1-4424-5080-6 $5.99
978-1-4424-5081-3 (eBook)

Katie and the Cupcake War

978-1-4424-5373-9 $5.99
978-1-4424-5374-6 (eBook)

Mia's Boiling Point

978-1-4424-5396-8 $5.99
978-1-4424-5397-5 (eBook)